D7

D1559489

Ex Libris

A BASKET OF HERBS

A BASKET OF HERBS

A Book of
American Sentiments

ILLUSTRATED BY

TASHA TUDOR

PRESENTED BY

THE NEW ENGLAND UNIT, INC.,
OF THE HERB SOCIETY OF AMERICA, INC.

EDITED BY

MARY MASON CAMPBELL, DEBORAH WEBSTER GREELEY,
PRISCILLA SAWYER LORD, AND ELISABETH W. MORSS

THE STEPHEN GREENE PRESS
Brattleboro, Vermont
Lexington, Massachusetts

This book is manufactured in the United States of America. It is published by The Stephen Greene Press, Fessenden Road, Brattleboro, Vermont 05301.

Library of Congress Cataloging in Publication Data

Main entry under title:

A Basket of herbs.

  Bibliography.
  1. Herbs—United States—Miscellanea.   I. Campbell, Mary Mason.   II. Tudor, Tasha.   III. Herb Society of America.   New England Unit.
QK98.4.U6B33   1983   582'.06'3   82–21130
ISBN 0–8289–0500–2

This book is dedicated to
Herb Lovers Everywhere

"For Use and for Delight"

The New England Unit, Inc., of The
Herb Society of America, Inc. especially
thanks Tasha Tudor for her gracious
gift of illustrations.

If the herb gardener collects the facts and fancies connected with his plants, unusual superstitions, legends and uses, and verifies their authenticity, he helps to preserve a wealth of material before, in our modern rushing days, all is lost in the oblivion of a less exciting past. Here let it be emphasized that no detail is too trivial or homely if it adds to the knowledge and understanding of the tremendously important part that herbs and their uses have played in the lives of all people.

—HELEN NOYES WEBSTER,
from *Herbs, How To Grow Them and How To Use Them.*

Contents

Illustrations

These are full-page illustrations appearing within the text.

Foreword

The gift of *A Basket of Herbs* or a Tussie-Mussie has greater meaning when it is accompanied by a message to indicate something of the history, the lore, the traditional symbols or the sentimental significance of the herbs and flowers which it contains.

Since the first settlers came to the shores of America, many with a talent for expression and a love of plants have been singing the praises of herbs. This book has gathered some of those praises in the hope that they may enhance with words of beauty and clarity the gift of *A Basket of Herbs*.

Perhaps the reader will be inspired to compose his or her own lines of special meaning given the herbal literary background here set forth. Whether or not this be true, these thoughts from American authors and poets are worth noting well, for in themselves they add to that history, lore, traditional symbolism, and sentimental significance of herbs.

LEMON VERBENA, LAVENDER, LADIES DELIGHTS, ROSE

The Herbs

ALOE

Aloe barbadensis (formerly *Aloe vera*); *Liliaceae*
"Healing, protection, grief, bitterness, patience, affection"

As is true of many herbs, Aloe *has come to have multiple symbolic meanings through its associations and uses by mankind. "As bitter as Aloes" is an old proverb. The herb has been used since ancient times to heal burns and small cuts, and as medicine for sick animals. Aloe was listed in the Song of Solomon. Once dedicated to Zeus and Jupiter, Aloe was also a religious symbol in Mideast countries. It was superstitiously believed to keep evil spirits away if a sprig were hung over the threshold.*

> In climes beneath the solar ray
> Where beams intolerable day,
> And arid plains in silence spread,
> The pale green *Aloe* lifts its head—
> The mystic branch at Moslem's door
> Betokens travel long and sore
> In Mecca's weary pilgrimage.
> —*Flora's Interpreter*

* * *

In Africa, their (*Aloe veras'*) native home, the land is aflame with the red and yellow spikes of the tubular blossoms from October to April.

Over two hundred species are known, varying from tiny stemless rosettes, through trailers, climbers and shrubs, to tree forms many feet high. . . . Grown as a pot plant, Aloe vera is . . . a convenience to a plant-loving housewife, for its rich green pulp does afford almost instant relief to a kitchen burn. . . . In time, Aloe vera may become a problem child, as its leaves are long and heavy and its adult height approaches two feet with a possible flower-stalk a foot higher. Probably by then it has reached retirement age, letting its children and grandchildren carry on.

—HELEN T. BATCHELDER,
The Herbarist 1964

* * *

A pot-plant, too tender to live outdoors except in tropical climes, Aloe vera asks very little of the gardener. Though the juice of the leaves relieves sunburn, the plant does not flourish in direct sunlight.

—GERTRUDE B. FOSTER

ANGELICA

Angelica Archangelica; Umbelliferae

"Inspiration, magic"

The names Angelica and Masterwort for this herb testify to old beliefs in its heavenly protective ability to cure all maladies and stop contagion. It was said to have been revealed by an angel in a dream, to cure the plague. While a symbol of inspiration and magic through the years, its principal use today is culinary; its taste and fragrance are delightfully aromatic. It is a native of cold countries where its reputation for enchantment and curative powers has long been warmly respected. Angelica is a favorite herb of confectioners and woodchucks.

In Lapland, Angelica has been used as a wreath to crown poets who fancy themselves inspired by its agreeable odor.

—CATHARINE H. WATERMAN

* * *

Then King Olaf entered,
Beautiful as morning,
Like the sun at Easter
   Shone his happy face;
In his hand he carried
Angelicas uprooted,
With delicious fragrance
   Filling all the place.

—HENRY WADSWORTH LONGFELLOW,
from "Tales of a Wayside Inn"

15

It seemed a shame to mar the perfect symmetry of this stately plant by cutting its stalks, but I was eager to try my hand at making from them some of the sweetmeats that were popular centuries ago. Very carefully I cut four long hollow stalks and took them to the kitchen to be candied. . . . I decorated a cake with them in the English fashion.

—ANNIE BURNHAM CARTER

* * *

Dear Elisabeth,
Although "I cannot come"
I will come
On the wings
Of the swallows,
My arms
Will be filled
With Angelica
And the sweetest and shyest
May Flower
From Arbutus Hill
Will be hiding
Somewhere
—there.

Love,
Margaret

—MARGARET THOMAS
Answer to an invitation

ARTEMISIA

MUGWORT: A. *vulgaris*

SOUTHERNWOOD: A. *abrotanum*

TARRAGON: A. *Dracunculus var. sativa*

WORMWOOD: (Common) A. *Absinthium*

Compositae

Herbarists are well acquainted with these four Artemisias. We find Artemisias by the roadside, in the fields, by the seashore, in gardens, on the prairies, even in the deserts of our own country. For centuries, the Artemisias have had many garden and household uses the world over. In kitchen gardens, Tarragon has been an indispensable member of the family. Abounding in symbols and meanings, the histories of these plants show them to have been in close relationship with gods and people. They were named for Artemis, the Greek goddess of the chase, who had great powers of magic. Myths, legends and stories of witchcraft have surrounded them always.

The gray foliage of artemisia brings a soft cloudy or misty look which intensifies the depth of greens in mints and savories, the pink in carnations and the violet in lavenders. The effect is similar to a rainy day when colors appear brighter than when the sun shines.

—HELEN MORGENTHAU FOX

MUGWORT

"Travel, happiness, tranquillity; 'Be Not Weary' "

Often now considered a common weed, Mugwort has nevertheless been a treasured herb for centuries. In addition to its most familiar name, Mugwort has been called Felon Herb, Sailor's Tobacco, Green Ginger, and Ghost-plant for reasons which are not difficult to understand. Since it was once considered to have immense powers over evil spirits, Mugwort was made into garlands on St. John's Day and was sometimes called St. John's Herb and St. John's Girdle. Because it was used to flavor drinks, including a type of beer, Mugwort became its most familiar name, from the vessel from which the drink was consumed. The herb was considered useful in preventing sunstroke, disease and misfortune, and in frightening wild beasts and insects—hence its use as a moth repellant. Since the time of the Crusades, a sprig of Mugwort worn in the shoe has been said to give one the power to walk without weariness. At least one runner in the Boston Marathon is known to have worn Mugwort in her shoe.

For a long time I have wanted to grow Mugwort. . . . The leaves, like the needle of the compass, turn towards the north and thus are thought to have magnetic influence. Crystal gazers used it to assist them in clairvoyance.

—ANNIE BURNHAM CARTER

* * *

Many plants that began to run wild [in America] had been cherished flowers or vegetables in Old World gardens. The settlers brought with them seeds or rooted pieces of the plants they were accustomed to grow for ornament and food and medicine. Many of these now grow wild in

the United States, and some, like . . . mugwort . . . are vigorous enough
to make their way into city lots.

—ANNE OPHELIA DOWDEN

* * *

. . . the annual sweet Mugwort, a tall, soft green feathery plant, with
a lovely fragrance and little whirling balls for flowers. It has a way of appearing in the gardens of people who have not planted it, and so de-
lighting them that they will travel a hundred miles to find out what it is.
It is the travelers' herb. A sprig in the shoe insures a safe journey.

—DOROTHY BOVÉE JONES

* * *

SOUTHERNWOOD

"Constancy, jest, bantering"

*Known as the Lover's Plant, Southernwood has been an emblem of con-
stancy and perseverance, with familiar names such as Lad's Love, Sweet
Benjamin, Old Man, and, curiously, Maiden's Ruin. The French name,*
Garde Robe, *refers to its household use protecting clothing from insects.*

Southernwood should always be planted at a spot where people stop,
whether to look at something or to talk. Then the experienced gardener's
hand goes out to nip off a bit of the tasselled foliage. Whether you are
standing to look at a garden or a view or are standing just to talk to a
friend or neighbor, you can crush the finely dissected leaves gently and
sniff their very special fragrance.

—BUCKNER HOLLINGSWORTH

I found the little packages on the kitchen table. There was a quaint West Indian basket which I knew its owner had valued, and which I had once admired; there was an affecting provision laid beside it for my seafaring supper, with a neatly tied bunch of southernwood and a twig of bay.

—SARAH ORNE JEWETT

* * *

Southernwood . . . is a fit neighbor for Chinese philosophers discussing life and poetry by a pool.

—HENRY BESTON

* * *

Pursuing the "neglect" method, Southernwood unharvested, planted hedgewise, provides a welcome feathery green on the landscape at a late summer date when fields all around are seared from the heat and rainless weeks.

—SISTER MARY MARGARET O.C.D.

* * *

Southernwood bears a balmier breath than is ever borne by many blossoms, for it is sweet with the fragrance of memory. The scent that has been loved for centuries, the leaves that have been pressed to the hearts of fair maids, as they questioned of love, are indeed endeared. . . .

—ALICE MORSE EARLE

TARRAGON

"Lasting interest, appeal, seduction"

No kitchen or windowsill herb garden is complete without the delightful French Tarragon, which does not set seed and seems to flourish best when slips are passed from gardener to gardener. Little is known about its ancient past. Its old-fashioned name, "Little Dragon" (from the Latin dracunculus)*, comes because it strangles itself with its own roots if not divided and separated every few years. Beloved of good cooks, French Tarragon is an herb of many culinary uses; it has indeed "lasting interest" to the taste, and is itself as appealing and seductive as its symbolisms imply.*

I am surprised how little legend and folk-lore is written about this herb. I have never seen it listed among the witches' herbs. Yet with a plant so bewildering and mysterious and having its name [dragon] derived from the roots being likened to the coil of a serpent, one wonders why the witches ignored it. Perhaps all its magic lies in its distinctive flavor, and as such I am content to have it at the top of my list.

—NANETTE M. STRAYER

* * *

The cultivated tarragon is only one of several instances in which a sterile but horticulturally superior variety of a garden herb has been spread around the world by vegetative propagation. . . . Just so did the man from whom we had the herb, and the man from whom *he* had it, and the man from whom *he* had it, and the man—. It was indeed by a series of just such steps that the cultivated tarragon spread out of its original Asiatic home and across central Europe and finally around the world.

—EDGAR ANDERSON

Tarragon or Astragon Vinegar: Pick the tarragon nicely from the stem, let it lie in a dry place forty-eight hours; put it in a pitcher, and to one quart of the leaves put three pints of strong vinegar; cover it close, and let it stand a week—then strain it, and after standing in the pitcher till quite clear, bottle it, and cork it closely.

—MRS. MARY RANDOLPH

* * *

J. Mason presents his respects to the President, and with very great pleasure . . . begs his acceptance of . . . Estragon, from the plant the President was so good as to send J. M. a year or two ago, which has flourished well in the open air—and will in Spring afford plenty of slips.

—GENERAL JOHN MASON,
from a letter to Thomas Jefferson,
January 22, 1809

* * *

WORMWOOD

"Absence, displeasure, bitterness"

As long ago as Biblical times, Wormwood has stood for all that was bitter and troubling to man. In less worrisome days, Wormwood was considered to be effective in healing bruises and other ills, and was often served to winners of strenuous athletic contests as a drink. Although for centuries it has had many medicinal, household and garden uses, today Wormwood is grown in gardens principally for its ornamental silver-grey effect. Its aromatic leaves are useful in flower arrangements, sachets, and moth bags. A Bible garden could not be complete without its plant of Wormwood.

You can always live well in any wild place by the sea . . . there was a few herbs in case she needed them. . . . A plant o' wormwood I remember seeing once when I stayed there. . . . Yes, I recall the wormwood, which is always a planted herb. . . . A growin' bush makes the best gravestone; I expect that wormwood always stood for somebody's solemn monument.

—SARAH ORNE JEWETT

* * *

There grew . . . the green wormwood whose leaves the priestesses of Isis had worn. Margaret loved best of all to work there in mid-morning when the gathering heat of the sun drew up the many strong fragrances of the leaves and the bees filled the air with their humming.

—ELIZABETH COATSWORTH

BALM – LEMON BALM

Melissa officinalis; Labiatae

"Sympathy, rejuvenation"

Although an Arabic symbol of rejuvenation, Balm was also believed in early times to make the heart merry and joyful; and to many, the herb is a traditional gesture of sympathy and love. In 17th-century America, it was believed that an essence of Balm drunk each morning would renew youth, strengthen the brain, relieve a "languishing nature," prevent baldness and gout, and relieve the sting of bees. Wearing Balm would make one loved by another, and drinking it as tea would insure a long life. Its fragrance made it a valuable "strewing herb" to freshen rooms. Today we use it in fruit cups, punches, teas and salads, and potpourris. It has been variously called Balm, Lemon Balm, Sweet Balm, and Balm Gentle.

It is on account of the soothing qualities of the waters distilled from this plant that it has been made the emblem of sympathy.

—CATHERINE H. WATERMAN

* * *

No plant of the garden has a better classical pedigree, and there is even a possible mention in the Odyssey. To the ancients a plant of fragrance and the source of a healing balsam, Balm is now a time-honoured presence whose medical fame has waned, but whose standing as a fragrance and an herb of gardens is perhaps higher than ever before. . . . The grown plant is not so much a bush as a lodge of leafy branches, some erect, others sloped off, all crisp and clean, all fragrant with a good and earthy smell of lemon. It is by the leaves of Balm that I find myself pausing when I chance to visit the garden in the morning when the plant faces the eastern sun. All nature is full of subtleties of light, and nowhere are they to be better seen than on the wings of birds and the surfaces of leaves.

—HENRY BESTON

* * *

The platforms on which bee skeps stood were scoured with branches of lemon balm in the 17th century to attract any errant swarm. Today bee keepers grow lemon balm for its high yield of nectar. . . . Rubbing fresh lemon balm on wooden furniture gives it a good gloss and delicious fresh scent. The oils in the herb foliage do the wood as much good as commercial lemon oil polish.

—GERTRUDE B. FOSTER

* * *

Lemon balm to cheer the bee,
Lemon balm in fruits and tea,
Lemon balm for sympathy . . .
—ELISABETH W. MORSS

* * *

The charm of balm as a garden plant, aside from its interesting history, is the delicious lemony, minty scent from its leaves. If grown on a bank where one can stroke it in passing, it is always a delight to sniff its fragrance on one's fingers.

—HELEN MORGENTHAU FOX

BASIL

Ocimum Basilicum; Labiatae

"Good wishes, love"

There are different kinds of Basil, and occasionally one may produce several kinds in the garden from a single packet of seed. The herb has always been of mystical and sentimental importance, as its history will show. In Greece, its name meant Royal, or King; in Crete, it symbolized "Love washed with tears." Today we think of it as an herb of love for its traditions in Italy of being shared by lovers. In India it is a holy herb, a charm against all misfortune. A strewing herb in mediaeval Europe, it has also long been used in the kitchen. Once it was believed that a Basil leaf buried with the dead was a passport to Heaven. Basil is effective in the kitchen garden, the kitchen, the flower garden, or the herb garden, and in a flower arrangement. It is always a welcome addition to a savory bouquet garni carried in a basket to one's hostess.

If of my Basils I have talked too much . . . I offer no apology, but the assurance that if I am privileged to share any of them with my readers they will do likewise.

—HELEN NOYES WEBSTER,
The Herbarist, 1936

* * *

One of the most balmy and beautiful of all the sweet breaths borne by leaves or blossoms is that of Basil. . . . Peasant girls always place

Basil in their hair when they go to meet their sweethearts, and an offered sprig of Basil is a love declaration. . . . The house surrounded by Basil is blessed, and all who cherish the plant are sure of heaven.

—ALICE MORSE EARLE

* * *

Whenever I walk among the herbs at noon, at that hour when a Spanish country saying will have it that the forces of the earth are at their exaltation of power, I can never pass one of the great Basils in the sun without a thought beginning there of the fantastic wonder of the whole green life of earth.

—HENRY BESTON

* * *

Sweet basil, with the most vivid green of all the herbs, is now in bloom. This oriental plant has a very intriguing smell, one that is strong of cloves. I feel there is a touch of mystery about it, as though the herb long ago in its native land of India, had absorbed the strange incense of some Hindu temple. . . . The history of this herb is full of conflicting superstitions. In ancient Greece it was an herb of hate, in Italy the . . . flower of lovers, immortalized by poets and painters.

—ANNIE BURNHAM CARTER

* * *

Sweet Purple Bush—the tiny purple flowers are always humming with honey bees which in their zeal bend the little bushes to the ground. Their fragrance combines all the odors of eastern spices. Do its leaves like those of Green Basil cure deafness when laid in the ears, make sweeter washing waters, or more potent medicinal oils? All this I do not know, but in sweet nosegays it excels.

—HELEN NOYES WEBSTER,
The Herbarist 1936

St. Michael's Day, September 29, is a delightful time for a party. There is a hint of autumn in the air though days are still warm and sunny. Basil rows are full and fragrant in the sun, green and purple against the long background of gray artemisias.

—ADELMA G. SIMMONS

BAY – SWEET BAY

Laurus nobilis; Lauraceae

"Glory, reward"

Variously known as Sweet Bay, Green Bay, True Laurel, Roman Laurel, or Grecian Laurel, this fabled plant symbolizes triumph and victory, eternity (Bay leaves do not wilt), chastity, glory, honor, success and renown, luck and pride. A sprig of Sweet Bay was a reward of merit, and once was used to ward off witches, devils, thunder, lightning, and defeat. The Greeks and Romans made wreaths of it to honor kings, priests, prophets and poets, victors in battle, scholarly and athletic contests—and so were coined such phrases as "poet laureate"; baccalaureate; "Look to your laurels"; "crowned with laurel." A sprig in a tussie mussie means "I shall conquer you." The herb was sacred to Apollo and Aesculapius in Roman times, and it has now come to be a favorite church green, a symbol of the Virgin Mary, a Christian symbol of triumph, eternity and chastity. A necessary part of a culinary bouquet garni, Laurus nobilis or Sweet Bay is also a charming fragrant green addition to a Basket of Herbs for the kitchen or the welcoming hand of a friend.

[A proverb for cooking:] Walk carefully around a bay leaf before you use a whole one.

—HELEN NOYES WEBSTER

SWEET BAY

Once a year I cut my twenty-year-old bay plant to take some foliage to our church. The shrub, now five feet tall, was nursed through cold winters in my house and then in a deep cold-frame. The first Sunday in Advent I have the privilege of putting herbs on the altar, and our rector always mentions the delight of smelling the pungent bay as he stands near the pewter vases holding the herbs. The warmth of the candles releases the scent.

—GERTRUDE B. FOSTER

* * *

I send you much love and many a thought, and I wish that I could put half the things into this letter that you would like to read and I to write. But you must take this leaf of Bay instead.

—CELIA THAXTER,
from a letter to her friend Mrs.
Whitman, April 15, 1900

* * *

[Early Western settlers noted similarities of *Laurus nobilis* to] . . . The waxy, fragrant California laurel, *Umbellularia californica* [which] was brought in from the canyons because it was the symbol of security. Danger and trouble could not harm one who dwelt beside it. Moreover, it afforded its bay leaves for flavoring, and its beautifully mottled wood for cabinetwork.

—CHARLES G. ADAMS

BEEBALM – BERGAMOT

Monarda didyma fistulosa, M. fistulosa

Labiatae

"Sweet virtues"

Beebalm was one of the earliest American native wildflowers to be taken into colonial gardens, where it was also variously known as Fragrant Balm, Crimson Balm, Wild Bergamot, Indian Plume, Oswego Tea, and, humorously, "Johnny-Pants-Pocket" because of the tiny "pocket" each petal contains. Although its principal values were its beauty in field and garden, and its sweet minty flavor in tea, Beebalm also came to have the meaning of sweet virtues in sentimental nosegays. An herb beloved by native American Indians and by colonists as well as by today's gardeners, it is also beloved by bees, hummingbirds, and butterflies.

In the limestone valley where we live, one of the most gorgeous sights of mid-summer is the mass of lavender produced by the truly native Bee Balm, *Monarda fistulosa* . . . it grows in pastures and on rocky hillsides. The early settlers learned to make tea of the dried leaves, possibly from the Indians. The undulating hills of our corner of Connecticut were occupied by tribes of Indians before the Dutch and the English.

—GERTRUDE B. FOSTER

* * *

Oswego tea, also known as bee balm or red bergamot, is a true American wildflower and like other mints, its native habitats are moist areas and stream banks. . . . Their tousled heads are most attractive in bouquets with daisies.

—BARBARA POND

BORAGE

Borago officinalis; Boraginaceae

"Courage"

For centuries, since before the Crusades, Borage was known as the herb of courage, and so it remains today. In addition to this, it came also to have a sentimental meaning of merriment. It has had virtues in medicine, and of flavor and beauty in garnishing cakes, salads, and beverages. It has also been called Bee Bread, Star Flower, Talewort, and Cool-Tankard. According to old wives' tales, Borage was sometimes smuggled into the drink of prospective husbands to give them the courage to propose marriage. Ego borago gaudia semper ago: "I, borage, always bring courage."

In all the plant realm, there is no more beautiful blue than that of the borage flower with its dancing starlike blooms.

—PRISCILLA SAWYER LORD

* * *

The day the heaped, round basket-trays of blue borage stars went on sale, what joyous fingering and poking, for just one old blossom with viable black contents in its hairy little pepper shaker. Two blossoms were found; enough, as it happened to provide a whole barrio with borage seedlings.

—ELEANOR CARROLL BRUNNER

Never before, perhaps, was such a sight—
Only one sky (my breath!) and all that blue—
Lapis, and Sevres, and borage—every hue
Of blue-jay—indigo bunting—bluebird's flight.
                    —EDNA ST. VINCENT MILLAY,
                    "Indigo Bunting"

* * *

Looking upward in a friend's terraced herb garden one summer day, I beheld a heavenly cloud of azure blue flower-stars, some pinkish, against a bluer sky. With the bees softly buzzing . . . what a sight! Her borage had reseeded itself.

                    —GENEVIEVE G. JYUROVAT

* * *

I am told that, "Borage is for merriment." I am brought to frustration by this declaration. . . . It is clear that for reasons now unknown to the messenger, borage is endowed with some kind of charismatic power. And that's that.

                    —KATHERINE I. AND H. B. FREDMAN

BURNET

Sanguisorba officinalis (Salad Burnet, *Poterium Sanguisorba*)

Rosaceae

"A merry heart"
Once called "God's little bird" because of its paired, picot-edged leaves
resembling wings, Burnet has also been known as "Salad Burnet" for its
cucumber-like taste and the use of the crisp leaves in green salads. Leaves
were said to make the heart merry, especially when added to a glass of
wine. Known in earliest American colonial days as a pot and salad herb,
it was also used as forage for sheep and cattle. It is at its charming best in
a tussie-mussie.

I have just received a letter from Majr. Flood informing me that his
neighbor Mr. Duval will spare me from 6. to 8. bushels of Burnet seed.
you will therefore be pleased to send off two boys on horseback to bring
it. they should take bags which will hold 4 bushels each. the seed is as
light as chaff. it is sown half a bushel to the acre.

—THOMAS JEFFERSON,
from a letter to Jeremiah Goodman,
February 21, 1812

Burnet, like alchemilla,
Rewards an early rising,
And even if you've seen them,
Its diamonds are surprising.
—ELISABETH W. MORSS,
"Salad Burnet"

* * *

The dusky flowers of salad burnet are out. It is a neat and charming herb and my group of three plants has remained unchanged in appearance and growth during the four years in which I have had them. The flowers are like round buttons of pink chenille which darken to a red brown as they age. The leaves are very pretty, notched sharply on the margins, soft to the touch, and in the pinnate form of a feather. The "poterium" (goblet or beaker) of its botanical name hints of its use in tankards of ale.
—ANNIE BURNHAM CARTER

CALENDULA

Calendula officinalis; Compositae

"Grief, despair"

Often known as Marigold or Pot Marigold, the Calendula has other common names going back to mediaeval times, such as Husbandman's Dyall ("Dial"), Flora's Clock, Johnny-Go-to-Bed-at-Noon, Marybud, Gold Bloom, and Marygold. Ancient herbalists knew this plant to be useful in cookery and medicine, as a dye plant for fabric and food, and in the garden. Its habit of opening in the sunshine and closing at sunset has given it many country connotations as a time-keeper. Its botanical name "Calendula" signifies that it is in bloom every month of the Roman calendar year in suitable climates. This golden-hued flower crossed the Atlantic with some of our first European settlers, and in 1672 John Josselyn reported that marigolds were thriving in the New World. One wonders why such a golden cheerful flower should always have had a meaning of grief and despair.

Calendula officinalis—Pot Marigold. A hardy annual, common to the gardens time out of mind, and formerly much used in soups and broths. Flowers deep orange, and continue all season.

—JOSEPH BRECK

* * *

The pot marigold is the single, annual calendula which is the ancestor of all the double ruffled giant calendulas which grow in many gardens. It is a modest plant, dear to herb growers because of its long history of culinary and medicinal use, because it blooms all summer, and because of its many literary associations. It is the only calendula which belongs in the herb garden.

—DOROTHY BOVÉE JONES,
The Herbarist 1962

* * *

Catharine Parr Traill, in the numerous editions of her book for prospective emigrants (Toronto, 1862), urged women to take with them plenty of seeds of useful plants, especially marigolds. These she had found to be effective in treating cuts, burns, bruises and gangrene. In her opinion, marigolds were the finest coloring matter for butter and cheese and one of the best yellow dyes for wool.

—EUSTELLA LANGDON

CELANDINE

Chelidonium majus; Papaveraceae

"Joys to come"

The botanical name for this old-fashioned herb came to us from Greece, where it meant "swallow" because it flowers when the swallows arrive in spring; it is also occasionally called "Swallow-wort." It was once believed to have qualities of bringing youth to old people who partook of its essence. Grown in Colonial gardens, it has now become naturalized in American fields and roadsides. A double-flowering form enhances modern gardens.

Celandine once graced Colonial gardens for both its beauty and its usefulness . . . today its prime value is for the production of yellow dye for wool. This attractive plant should be welcomed back to shady gardens because it grows easily and blooms over a long period of time.

—BARBARA POND

* * *

Careless of its neighborhood, we see its pleasant face in wood and meadow, in the rustic lane and in the stately avenue, on the princely domain and in the meanest place upon the highway.

—WILSON FLAGG

* * *

There has never been a time in history when people did not need plants to cheer them and even one's commonest weeds become respected herbs if you know their background of service and sentiment which caused plants which we consider wildlings to be carried across the ocean with the early settlers. Celandine, with its bright yellow petals and orange juice in the white stems, which suggested to early physicians that it was a specific for jaundice, is something I weed out of every garden bed. I do it with some deference and leave a little to seed along the edge of the woods.

—GERTRUDE B. FOSTER

CHAMOMILE

Chamaemelum nobile; Compositae

"Wisdom, patience, long life, energy in adversity"

Well known for centuries, Chamomile is rich in its reputation for alleviating miseries, weariness, and many ills, especially when drunk in an aromatic tea. It has also been used in olden times as a strewing herb, a flavoring for wines and liqueurs, and in gardens to keep its plant neighbors healthy. It has been planted purposely in garden walks because Chamomile has little objection to being trodden upon, a characteristic which has resulted in its being the emblem of "energy in adversity."

In old gardens, seats made of raised earth . . . were covered with the mossy-looking chamomile. There is an old belief that if chamomile is dispersed about the garden it will keep the plants healthy.

—HELEN MORGENTHAU FOX

* * *

During the war of the Revolution, a British officer, walking in one of our gardens, eagerly inquired the names of the plants therein cultivated. Coming to a bed of flourishing chamomile, he asked the lady, mistress of the grounds, who attended him with evident reluctance, what was the name of that low plant.

"The Rebel's Flower," replied she, with firmness. "Why so called," questioned the officer. "Because," was the distinct and bold reply, "it flourishes the more, the more it is trampled upon."

—MISS S. C. EDGARTON

41

CHERVIL

Anthriscus Cerefolium; Umbelliferae

"Sincerity; 'Warms old hearts' "

Chervil's botanical name "Anthriscus" comes from the Greek word mean-ing "flower" and "fence"; "cerefolium" means "leaf of Ceres," referring to the fragrant joy-giving leaves, which "warm old hearts." Although this herb has little history of magic, it has long been cultivated in gardens by those who have an affection for its delicate beauty and light anise flavor. Peter Kalm, traveling in America in 1749, found wild chervil, which he said "abounds in all the woods in North America." Of special interest in culinary gardens, chervil is one of the French fines herbes. It is pretty in bouquets, and, when dried, it adds delicate fragrance to a potpourri.

As compared with other herbs of ancient fame, descriptions of chervils are brief and singularly free from folklore, magic and imaginary medical virtues. . . . Happily, however, today's awakened interest in herb-gardening and appreciation of the delicate herb-blending so long an art in French cookery, admits at least our salad chervil . . . to its rightful place among the aristocrats of seasoning.

—HELEN NOYES WEBSTER,
The Herbarist 1947

* * *

Chervil is the noble cousin of the parsleys. The flavor of chervil is so tender that it should be used more generously than other herbs.

—LEONIE DE SOUNIN

42

Chervil is a very pretty addition to delicate flower arrangements, of particular charm in the old-fashioned nosegays called tussie-mussies, and an appetizing platter garnish. Chervil brings out the best in other herbs and foods with which it is combined, just as some charming people stimulate others about them.

—MARY MASON CAMPBELL

CHIVES

Allium Schoenoprasum; Amaryllidaceae

"Usefulness"

One cannot dispute that the symbolism for garden Chives, "usefulness," is appropriate for this kitchen garden herb. Its pale purple flower is useful especially in gardens, flower arrangements, and salads. All parts of the plant have a mild onion flavor not entirely welcome in a tussie-mussie meant to be smelled, although bees find the blossoms inviting. Chives nevertheless have been of inestimable value as a food and are a welcome addition to a culinary Basket of Herbs.

March 29, 1806. (On the Columbia River, return journey.) Among the moss on the rocks we observed a species of small wild onions growing so closely together as to form a perfect turf, and equal in flavor to the shives of our gardens, which they resemble in appearance also.

—MERIWETHER LEWIS,
in *Lewis and Clark Journals*

* * *

"We needed something to flavor the caribou stew," he said, pointing to a great bed of . . . chives. "They grew along the banks of the Anderson about 60 miles east of the Mackenzie River, near the Beaufort Sea, and I collected the roots there."

—DOROTHY E. SWALES

Chives are nice in salad
To cheese, they give a zest,
Are very good in scrambled eggs
But I think I like them best
Growing as fringe in the garden
A trimming for flower beds
Like rows of little rushes
With dusty pinkish heads.

—L. YOUNG CORRETHERS,
"Chives"

CLOVER – RED CLOVER

Trifolium pratense; Leguminosae

"Dignity, industry, promise, good luck"

While Clovers as a family signify dignity, red Clover means industry; white, promise; and four-leaved Clovers always bring good luck, or mean "Be Mine"; while a five-leaved Clover is thought to bring bad luck. Through the magic power of a four-leaved Clover, the fairies may become visible. Symbols and meanings were given to Clover, and especially the four-leaved, by the ancient Celts and Druids, among whom it was held to be a sacred plant. To this day, a four-leaved Clover means good luck. Clover blossoms are beloved by the bees, and by children who make fragrant flower chains or use them to fill May baskets.

> One leaf for fame
> And one for wealth,
> One for a faithful lover
> And one to bring you glorious health—
> Are in a four-leaf clover.
>> —ANTHONY S. MERCATANTE

* * *

> In counterpoint
> Of clover and Queen Anne's lace
> Summer sings to me.
>> —LOIS O'CONNOR

Never expect a bee to be
Calm in blossomed clover.

—ROBERT PETER TRISTRAM COFFIN,
from "Small Bee in Clover"

* * *

It isn't raining rain to me,
But fields of clover bloom,
Where any buccaneering bee
Can find a bed and room.

—ROBERT LOVEMAN,
from "April Rain"

* * *

The pedigree of honey
Does not concern the bee;
A clover, any time, to him
Is aristocracy.

—EMILY DICKINSON

* * *

John Torrey, professor of botany and chairman of the greenhouse committee, made one lucky discovery some years ago when experimenting with clover development. After increasing the daily light from eight to sixteen hours . . . the result was a crop of four-leaf clovers.

—ANONYMOUS,
Harvard Today

COSTMARY

Chrysanthemum Balsamita; Compositae

"Sweetness, preservation"

The name of this sweet-herb comes from the Latin word "costus," meaning "Oriental plant"; and from "Mary" in reference to the Mother of Christ, or possibly to Mary Magdalene. Among its popular names are Alecost, because it was once used to give a spicy flavor to ale; Goose Tongue, Bible Leaf, Sweet-Mary, Sweet-Tongue, and Sage o'Bedlam. Long known as a strewing herb, it has also been used for a fragrant tea, a soothing addition to a bath, and in potpourri. Its most sentimental use in our country has been our grandmothers' habit of marking a place in their Bibles with the long, narrow, sweet-smelling leaf.

> "Costmary, Costmary,
>   How did you grow?"
> "The trade routes from Asia,
>   A long to and fro."
>
> "Costmary, Costmary,
>   What came with you?"
> "Healing and spicing
>   And sweet leaves to strew."
>   —ELISABETH W. MORSS,
>   "Costmary (Alecost)"

My curiosity about herbs goes back to 1898, to the time when my mother used to keep a pressed leaf as a book-mark in her Bible. She called the leaf *Bibel Blatt*. For many years, it was known to me only by that name; I had never seen a plant with any flowers to reveal its botanical identity. When at last I saw this same plant in bloom by a roadside in northern New York, the small yellow flower-heads told me at once that the Bible Leaf of my childhood was the old-fashioned herb, costmary.

—WALTER CONRAD MUENSCHER

* * *

The sun shone on the tiny yellow buttons of costmary. They remind me of the small glove buttons that as a child I liked to help my mother fasten with a silver buttonhook when she dressed for afternoon calls.

—ANNIE BURNHAM CARTER

* * *

Costmary . . . is delicious, at least to the nose. The long flaccid green leaves have a scent that is like that of no other herb but is vaguely reminiscent of the taste of "morning bitters" (whiskey with bitter herbs) that was a commonplace in many southern households a generation ago. It was a famous nibbling herb and played a part often in the Sabbath posy, or lay as a book-mark in the Bible or hymnal. . . . My country neighbors in Rockland County, N.Y., called it Sweet Mary Anne. . . . My root of Costmary came to me from a very old Germantown garden and I value it highly.

—LOUISE BEEBE WILDER

CROCUS, SAFFRON

Crocus sativus; Iridaceae

"Mirth, cheerfulness"

Treasured for its fragrance, flavor and color, Saffron Crocus has been cultivated for centuries. It gave its name to a town in England long ago, Saffron Walden. It provides a dye color of particular beauty, and flavoring is made of its stigmas, useful especially in bread, cake, soups, rice and fish dishes. The traditional meanings of cheerfulness and mirth come from the sunny golden color so apparent in its uses.

One finds in the Museum of Heraklion [Greece] a beautiful fresco of the saffron gatherer, and the flower blooms in many parts of Attica.

—MARY LINES WELLMAN

* * *

October. The saffron crocus along the brick edging of the borders is lovely now with its pale purple flowers. . . . Three orange stigmas hang from behind the petals. The stigmas, when dried, yield a rich powder which is used in cookery, and was once used in medicine, and to color the satin robes and slippers of the Persian kings and dye the hair of the women. The powder was much in demand for coloring fancy desserts and other dishes.

—ANNIE BURNHAM CARTER

In late October, when the frosts have blighted the dahlias, it is a delight to come upon the delicate grayish-purple blossoms [of Saffron Crocus] so like the first crocuses of spring, in the otherwise devastated garden.

—HELEN MORGENTHAU FOX

* * *

. . . [S]peculation aside, we can place saffron almost as far back as we can find evidence of civilization.

—BUCKNER HOLLINGSWORTH

DANDELION

Taraxacum Leontodon; Compositae

"Depart! Rustic oracle"

Especially beloved of children and bees, the Dandelion is not so popular with farmers and gardeners, except possibly for its use as a pot or salad herb in the early spring, or for making wine from its blossoms. The name comes from the French "dent de lion," or lion's tooth, referring to the long jagged shape of its leaf. Its meaning, "depart," undoubtedly comes from the farmers' wishes concerning its presence in the fields. A second meaning, "rustic oracle," may have come from childrens' belief that when a blossom is rubbed under the chin, pollen left there tells whether one likes butter (everyone does!); also, by blowing the seed-heads, one can tell what time it is, or how many children one will have when grown up.

Long considered beneficial, a source of food and medicine, dandelions continue to serve mankind, principally by enriching those who manufacture weed-killers. But dyers, wine-makers and imaginative cooks still gather the leaves, roots and flowers, using all parts of this persistent herb. . . . Like snow, dandelions enchant children but dismay adults.

—BARBARA POND

Simple and fresh and fair from winter's close
    emerging,
As if no artifice of fashion, business, politics, had ever
    been,
Forth from its sunny nook of shelter'd grass—
    innocent, golden, calm as the dawn,
The spring's first dandelion shows its trustful face.

             —WALT WHITMAN,
             "The First Dandelion"

* * *

. . . the dandelion lowers itself after flowering, and lies close to the ground while it is maturing its seed, and then rises up. After flowering, retired from society, as it were, meditates in seclusion; but after it lifts itself up again, the stalk begins anew to grow, it lengthens daily, keeping just above the grass till the fruit is ripened, and the little globe of silvery down is carried many inches higher than was the ring of golden flower. And the reason is obvious. The plant depends upon the wind to scatter its seeds; every one of these little vessels spreads a sail to the breeze, and it is necessary that they be launched above the grass and weeds. . . . It is a curious instance of foresight in a weed.

             —JOHN BURROUGHS

* * *

The approach of spring in our city parks is marked by the appearance of the Dandelion gatherers. It is always interesting to see, in May, on the closely guarded lawns and field expanses of our city parks, the hundreds of bareheaded, gayly-dressed Italian and Portugese women and children eagerly gathering the young Dandelion plants to add to their fare as a greatly-loved delicacy.

             —ALICE MORSE EARLE

Dear common flower, that grow'st beside the way,
Fringing the dusty road with harmless gold;
   First pledge of blithesome May,
Which children pluck, and full of pride, uphold,
   High-hearted buccaneers, o'erjoyed that they
An Eldorado in the grass have found,
   Which not the rich earth's ample round
May match in wealth, thou art more dear to me
Than all the prouder summer blooms may be.
                    —JAMES RUSSELL LOWELL,
                       from "To the Dandelion"

DILL

Anethum graveolens; Umbelliferae

"Preservation, good spirits"

Symbolically meaning "preservation," Dill is best known for its use in making pickles. It is also used extensively to flavor breads, salads, cookies, fish, eggs, and cheese. Its name perhaps comes from the old Norse word "dilla," which means "lull," referring to its ancient use to induce sleep. It was believed an absolute charm against witches and all their evils. Once used medicinally, it is now chiefly a culinary herb; its yellow flowers are charming in bouquets.

Dill . . . is one of the most beautiful and distinguished plants I think I have ever seen. It is a study in the elements of pure form and the qualities of delicacy and grace. . . . Dill is a plant of the old "Witchcraft."

—HENRY BESTON

* * *

Nice cheerful Dill—so easy to grow
Is a household friend; but did you know
That long ago, he played a part
As assistant to the Enchanter's art?
Well—times have changed,
Fortune is fickle
Now he provides the soul of a pickle.

—L. YOUNG CORRETHERS

DILL

Dill was used by the ancient Greeks and Romans to weave pungently fragrant garlands as crowns for the foreheads of their conquering heroes. Their poets sang its praises and grew lyrical over the feathery beauty of the dill branches forever springing anew in the gardens of Athens and Rome. Wreaths of the dark, dull yellow dill flowers were woven into decorations for the Romans' banquet halls. There the aromatic and half-unpleasant fragrance of the flowers seemed to cleanse the heavy air and permeate the spacious stuffy halls with the herb's spicy and peculiar freshness.

—MILO MILORADOVICH

ELDER

Sambucus canadensis; Caprifoliaceae

"Compassion, bad luck, zealousness"

Possibly no herb has had such a mystical, legendary past, and its works of magic against all evils are many. Known variously as Whitsunday Flower, Pipe Tree, and Popgun Tree (because of its pithy stems from which pipes, whistles, and popguns could be made), Elder's meanings vary from bad luck to good luck, compassion, zealousness, humility, and kindness. Druids thought that permission to cut an Elder tree must always be asked first of the spirit that lived in the tree. Who stands under an Elder at midnight on Midsummer's Eve shall see the King of Elves. Some countrymen believe that an Elder is never struck by lightning, and so plant it near the house for protection. Its powers against witchcraft are strong; its real uses as an herb include jelly, wine, tea, and pie, and as a coloring in dyes.

The healing elder, like compassion mild,
Lifts her meek flowers amid the pathless wild.
—SARAH JOSEPHA HALE

July 4th. Have pease for dinner, the first time. James L. prepares tea to the dry house. July 6th. Go after Elderflowers. Elder Flowers when green weigh 289 lbs. when dried 56 lbs.

—AMY BESS MILLER,
from a journal kept by the
deaconesses at New Lebanon, N.Y.

* * *

The elderberry which they called *Zauco* was planted to ward off evil spells which anyone who held a grudge could cast. A bit of it concealed on the person removed all power of evil. Besides the *Zauco* gave the quickest possible shade to the garden, and its berries could be brewed into a tasty wine.

—CHARLES G. ADAMS

FENNEL

Foeniculum vulgare; Umbelliferae

"Sorrow, strength, flattery; 'Worthy of praise' "

In common with many other herbs known in mediaeval days and even earlier, Fennel has a history linking it with devils and witchcraft, folk medicine, and culinary herbs. From root to seed, Fennel is valued even today for its aromatic, sweet, fragrant properties, with a taste reminiscent of anise. Its meanings are varied, a connotation of flattery being most often associated with it. A graceful plant, it is essential for a well-stocked kitchen garden, and its feathery leaves and flowers add delicacy to a Basket of Herbs.

. . . the Greek word *Marathon* means fennel, and the celebrated battle of Marathon, 490 B.C., was fought on a field of fennel.

—JESSICA WOOD

* * *

Above the lowly plants it towers,
The fennel, with its yellow flowers,
And in an earlier age than ours
Was gifted with the wondrous powers,
    Lost vision to restore.

It gave new strength, and fearless mood;
And gladiators, fierce and rude,
Mingled it in their daily food;
And he who battled and subdued,
    A wreath of fennel wore.
        —HENRY WADSWORTH LONGFELLOW,
        from "The Goblet of Life"

* * *

May 16, 1806. Shabonos [Touissant Charbonneau, the guide and interpreter] Squar ["squaw," *Sacajawea*] gathered a quantity of fenal roots which we find very paliatable and nurushing food. The onion we also find in abundance and boil it with our meat. . . .

Sunday 18th May 1806. The Squar wife to Shabono busied herself gathering the roots of the fenel called by the Snake Indians Year-pay [yampa, or squawroot, var. *Perideridia Gairdneri*] for the purpose of drying to eate on the Rocky mountains. those roots are very palatiable either fresh roasted boiled or dried and are generally between the size of a quill and that of a mans finger and about the length of the latter.

        —CAPTAIN WILLIAM CLARK, in
        Lewis and Clark Journals

* * *

It is said he [Johnny Appleseed] carried fennel seed . . . planted it, and urged others to do so. . . . Whether or not this is true, I want to believe it.

        —MARJORIE DOWNING

* * *

It was a universal custom among the elder folk to carry a Sunday posy; the stems were discreetly enwrapped with the folded handkerchief which also concealed the sprig of fennel.

        —ALICE MORSE EARLE

A serviceable thing
Is fennel, mint, or balm,
Kept in the thrifty calm
Of hollows, in the spring;
Or by old houses pent.

—LIZETTE WOODWORTH REESE,
from "Herbs"

FORGET-ME-NOT

Myosotis sylvatica, Boraginaceae

"Faithfulness, true love, forget-me-not"

Forget-Me-Not must surely be included in any list of flowers "for use and for delight" in bouquets, tussie-mussies, and gardens. Its traditional meanings have long been known among lovers, particularly during the Victorian era. The shape of its leaves has given this flower another common name, "Mouse-Ears." Anyone beginning a journey on February 29 should always be given a basket of Forget-Me-Nots, and the flowers should be exchanged on that day between friends for everlasting love and esteem. In the garden in spring, Forget-Me-Nots are a joy, always tucked into a Maybasket for one's true love.

Near the summit [of an Alaskan mountain] were patches of a most exquisite forget-me-not [var. *M. alpestris*] of a pure, delicate blue with yellow center. It grew to the height of a foot, and a handful of it looked like something just caught out of the sky above.

—JOHN BURROUGHS

You notice
as
the flowering spike
of the
forget-me-not
lengthens
with flowering it
leaves
behind a drab notation (namely
seeds even
smaller
than the flowers)
which does not
say
forget me not
because
it means to
be back

—A. R. AMMONS,
"Insouciance"

GERANIUM

Pelargonium (P. *graveolens*, Rose Geranium); *Geraniaceae*

"Preference, folly, stupidity; 'You are childish' "

While the "common" or zonal geranium has a traditional meaning of folly and is a bad-luck gift to a man, there ends the unsavory connotation of geraniums, for the many scented varieties reflect pleasure, happiness, and other virtues. The list of geraniums is long; it is said that at one time there were hundreds of varieties. Beloved of gardeners, who grow them for their beauty and fragrance, scented geraniums are often used in potpourris and bouquets, and at the teatable their leaves add flavor to the tea, cakes, cookies, or jelly. Rose Geraniums were known to our grandmothers in their parlors, gardens, and kitchens, and to their grandmothers before them.

These herbs of nostalgic memories now seem just right with rosewood lady chairs, pedestal center tables, and cabbage rose carpets, and their sentimental charms increase when we discover they even have a language of their own.

—HELEN VAN PELT WILSON

* * *

Scented geraniums in wide variety have merit for their unusual textures which vary from pebbly leaves to the delectable velvety feel of peppermint geranium. The range of leaf designs is almost unbelievable . . .

65

ROSE GERANIUM

from the tiny finger-bowl types to skeleton-leaved forms and the nearly round-leaved varieties.

—PRISCILLA SAWYER LORD

* * *

Our grandmothers knew well the "rose geraniums" and when the jar of apple jelly was filled, placed on the top [was] a leaf of the *graveolens* or skeleton-leaved, either of which when dried, is an addition to any pungent potpourri. But these are not plants to grow for use. They are for enchantment.

—ROSETTA E. CLARKSON

* * *

What kind of fragrance do you wish? Just name it and it's yours from the Pelargonium shelf—apple, lime, rose, lemon, peppermint, strawberry, cocoanut, apricot, nutmeg, almond . . . fantastic that from this one genus we have this choice, and more besides, in fragrance. Variety does not end here, for leaf form rivals fragrance. Broad, velvety green leaves; tiny satiny gray ones; those with deep rich green shiny lobes; oak leaves with handsome dark purple-black zones . . .

—DORCAS BRIGHAM

* * *

The pleasure of the fragrance of the leaves as they are touched is reason enough to grow scented geraniums. The fresh leaves can be placed in cake tins before baking, in jellies, in ice cream, in fruits and desserts. The dried leaves in many potpourris, sweet pillows and moth bags. Tussie mussies are bouquets of fragrant herbs, wonderful to take to invalids at home or in the hospital. The heat of their hands releases the scent of the herbs.

—CHARLOTTE ERICHSEN-BROWN

In the window recesses [in Thomas Jefferson's apartment in the White House], were stands for the flowers and plants which it was his delight to attend and among his roses and geraniums was suspended the cage of his favorite mockingbird.

—MRS. SAMUEL HARRISON SMITH

* * *

[. . . Of the herb Robert, a native wild Geranium:]

> Here, where the moors stretch free,
> In the high blue afternoon,
> Are the marching sun and talking sea
> And the racing winds that wheel and flee
> On the flying heels of June.
>
> Jill-o'er-the-ground is purple blue,
> Blue is the Quaker-Maid,
> The wild geranium holds its dew
> Long in the boulder's shade.

—WILLIAM VAUGHN MOODY,
from "Gloucester Moors"

GERMANDER

Teucrium Chamaedrys; Labiatae

"Facility, joy"

The meaning "Facility" for this ancient herb may have come from its use as a cure for gout, providing facility to anyone employing it successfully. From the earliest days of formal knot gardens, the plant has been used as a clipped edging to border the patterns of the knots. It was also used as a strewing herb and to indicate "Joy" in wreaths and tussiemussies. Both its leaves and flowers have a rich and pleasant fragrance. A single plant is easily layered to produce plants for borders.

[Of Herbs:]

They quilt the more informal beds,
  They wander wide
  Or primly bide.
They damask in a patterned pride,
  Germander-tied.
            —ELISABETH W. MORSS,
            from "The Gathering"

* * *

The green enclosures of Elizabethan days evidently overflowed with fragrant flowers, and the little beds in which they were confined were neatly edged with some sweet-leaved plant . . . Germander cut to a formal line.

—LOUISE BEEBE WILDER

GOLDENROD

Solidago canadensis, S. odora; Compositae

"Precaution, encouragement"

There are nearly a hundred varieties of Goldenrod found growing wild in America, any of which, used either fresh or dried, is a fragrant golden-flowered addition to a bouquet. A favorite herb of American Indians, Goldenrod was also used in medicine by the early colonists, who called it Woundwort. In addition to its use as a floral decoration, Goldenrod is widely used today as an herb dye plant, yielding a soft yellow color. In Europe, gardeners find our native Goldenrod an attractive background plant for flower borders, but it is so prolific in our own country that few use it thus here.

During the American Revolution, sweet goldenrod [sometimes] took the place of the English tea which the patriots had misplaced in Boston. The anise-flavored beverage was called Blue Mountain tea. Indians brewed a stronger infusion from Canadian goldenrod.

—BARBARA POND

* * *

I've decided to start a flower lobby of my own [for a National Flower]. . . . the humble but glorious goldenrod, which grows wild in every state of the Union and spreads its cheerful gold in August and September from Maine to the Pacific, from Canada to Florida and New Mexico. It is as sturdy and as various as our population; there is delicate dwarf goldenrod, silver goldenrod, tall yellow goldenrod in a multitude of forms and shapes—spikes, plumes, and panicles of native gold. . . . Descend into a bog and there, growing wild, is goldenrod; climb a mountain and there, between the crevices of boulders, is goldenrod; follow the shore of the sea and goldenrod gleams along the edge of the sands; drive along our highways from coast to coast in August and September and the fields and ditches are bright with goldenrod. . . . The goldenrod also has the great advantage—if it were to be our national flower—of owing nothing to man, of enriching no seed company . . . and of being as wild as our national bird, the eagle. . . . Who, for lack of a garden, hasn't gathered armfuls of goldenrod to bring cheer into a bleak summer cottage or camp? Who, even *with* a garden, hasn't put a jar of goldenrod on the porch in August?

—KATHARINE S. WHITE

* * *

October in New England,
And I not there to see
The glamour of the goldenrod,
The flame of the maple tree!

October in my own land . . .
I know what glory fills
The mountains of New Hampshire
And Massachusetts hills.

—ODELL SHEPARD,
"Home Thoughts"

Along the roadside, like the flowers of gold
That tawny Incas for their gardens wrought,
Heavy with sunshine droops the golden-rod.
            —JOHN GREENLEAF WHITTIER,
       from "Among the Hills'

HELIOTROPE

Heliotropium arborescens; Boraginaceae

"Eternal love, devoted attachment"

Heliotrope was so named by the Greeks because it turns ("tropos") to the sun ("helios") during the course of the day, turning again at dawn toward the rising sun. Thus it came to symbolize enduring and adoring love and admiration. In mythology and early medicine, it was an important herb. Sometimes called Simpler's Joy and All-Heal, its medicinal use has faded into the past, but its lavish fragrance makes it a valuable flower in bouquets and for the garden. Although the character of its fragrance is not easy to describe, some identify it with the smell of cherry pie, and so call it the Cherry-Pie Plant. Bees do not seem attracted to the flowers in spite of the fragrance.

Heliotrope. to be sowed in the spring. a delicious flower.

—THOMAS JEFFERSON

* * *

The odor of heliotrope, more than any other plant, can surround me with memories of other days, other times; can stir my imagination to scenes of . . . ladies receiving courtly gentlemen to afternoon tea, of an opera party in the 'nineties with guests in full regalia. . . . There is something intoxicating about the odor and I bury my nose again and again in the fragrant cluster, more memories, more scenes crowd around me. . . . The old-time, colloquial name for the plant was cherry pie, because of the almond-like odor found in cherry pits which was thought similar to that of heliotrope.

—ROSETTA E. CLARKSON

* * *

Heliotrope, a means to prevent calumniation. The virtues of this plant are miraculous if it be collected in the sign of the lion, in the month of August, and wrapped up in a laurel leaf together with the tooth of a wolf. Whoever carries this about with him, will never be addressed harshly by anyone, but all will speak to him kindly and peaceably. And if anything has been stolen from you put this under your head during the night, and you will surely see the whole figure of the thief. This has been found true.

—ANNE G. HAYWARD

HOLLY

Ilex Aquifolium, I. verticillata; Aquifoliaceae

"Life everlasting, good wishes, foresight, hope, divinity, festivity"

Everywhere it grows, Holly is rich in meaning, history, tradition, and the devotion of gardeners. It has found a firm place in nature, in gardens, and certainly in the lives and sentiments of humanity. Although "an herb of the fairies" (whom it has sheltered in winter when other trees were bare), it is known as the Holy Tree for its relationship to traditions of the Christian churches. Used as decorations, lustrous green holly branches and their bright berries bring cheer into homes and churches during all the Christmas season. A sprig carried home from a church service brings good luck. There are few rivals for its high place denoting festivity and good wishes.

The Cape Cod area is one of the places where English colonists first saw American holly and recognized it as a relative of one they had left behind in England. Hollies are native in that region and some trees now living may have been there when the Pilgrims landed in 1620.

—H. HAROLD HUME

* * *

The lore connected with holly is rich indeed and the superstitions most extraordinary. It was believed to be unlucky if holly were left up after New Year's or Twelfth Night, hence the burning of the greens. In this

75

case it was feared that spirits or ghosts might disturb the maidens of the household.

—DANIEL J. FOLEY

* * *

April 6, 1785: Sowed the semicircle North of the front gate with Holly Berries sent me by my Brother John—three drills of them: The middle one of Berries which had been got about Christmas and put in Sand, the other two of Berries which had been got earlier in the year, gently dried and packed in Shavings.

March 30, 1786: Planted . . . in my shrubbries a number of small holly trees which some months ago Colo. Lee of Stratford sent me in a box with earth. . . . I also planted several holly trees which had been sent to me the day before by a neighbor, Mr. Thos. Allison.

—GEORGE WASHINGTON

* * *

The ancient Romans sent sprigs of holly to their friends as a symbol of friendship, token of goodwill and wishes for good fortune. It is not surprising that holly is referred to in many old carols for its rich lively green in winter is a true symbol of life everlasting.

—HESTER METTLER CRAWFORD

* * *

Then sing to the holly, the Christmas holly,
   That hangs over peasant and king;
While we laugh and carouse 'neath its glittering
      boughs,
   To the Christmas holly we'll sing.

The gale may whistle, and frost may come
  To fetter the gurgling rill;
The woods may be bare and the warblers dumb—
  But the holly is beautiful still.

—ELIZA COOK

HOLLYHOCK

Alcea rosea; Malvaceae

"Ambition, liberality"

The very word "Hollyhock" conjures up mind pictures of white picket fences, old stone walls, red barns, and cottages by the sea. The herb is an ancient one, having been known in Greece before the birth of Christ, and it was used in mediaeval times as a medicine, a dye, and a fiber to be woven into cloth. Hollyhocks were truly one of the early American garden flowers, as John Josselyn mentioned them in his Voyages to New England *in the 17th century; and seeds were advertised for sale in a Boston newspaper in 1760. In China, Hollyhocks are a symbol of nature; in our country their manner of reaching for the sky gives them a meaning of ambition and a liberal nature.*

I have seen them in Connecticut growing wild—garden strays, standing up by ruined stone walls in a pasture with as much grace of grouping, as good form, as if they had been planted by our most skillful gardeners.

—ALICE MORSE EARLE

* * *

Mrs. Swune (that was not her real name, but she was a very real person) loved hollyhocks, and they did well in her garden. . . . Naturally, she became very hollyhock-conscious, and she wrote some poems about them and had her friends in for a sedate tea among the hollyhocks, and brought out the poems and read them. . . . It really wasn't as bad as it sounds; the poems were short and there were plenty of excellent tea-cakes, and the other guests were swell people and we kind of banded together. At the conclusion of the tea she presented each of us with a large packet of hollyhock seed and wanted to know if we would please scatter them through the Ozarks whenever we drove down that way. . . . What Mrs. Swune did not understand is that most plants are very choosy about where they will and will not grow.

—EDGAR ANDERSON

* * *

I think the eminently respectable Hollyhock must be doing a little boot-legging for I have often found a bumblebee completely undone within the capacious cup—the morning after.

—LOUISE BEEBE WILDER

* * *

The flower that has become synonymous with Marblehead was one that grew first, ages ago, in China where it flourished around beehives. It reached the western world close on the heels of the silk trade caravans. Hollyhocks soon made themselves at home in Marblehead. They grew like weeds, springing up along the narrow edges of the crooked sidewalks, behind fence posts, in the crevices of walls, among loose rocks. . . . By the fourth of July, there was hardly a picket fence or gateway or dooryard that did not have its share of hollyhocks in bloom. . . . After the turn of the nineteenth century, some poetic soul christened this old fishing com-munity "Hollyhock Town". . . . Tourists gathered seeds as they roamed about, put them in their purses and carried them home to Ashtabula, Sioux City, Independence, and elsewhere. . . .

—PRISCILLA SAWYER LORD

HOREHOUND

Marrubium vulgare; Labiatae

"Health"

One of the "bitter herbs" of the Bible, Horehound (sometimes spelled "Hoarhound") for centuries has been combined with honey or sugar as a pleasant antidote for coughs, and horehound candy can still be found for sale in old-fashioned candy shops. For the common cold, country people make a beneficial tea of Horehound leaves. Long known in Europe, Horehound was early introduced into America as a garden herb, and it became naturalized in some areas. A half-hardy perennial, it was listed for sale in the garden catalogs of some of our early plantsmen, including William Prince of Boston and John Bartram of Philadelphia. Shakers grew it, sold plants and seeds, and made candy and syrups of this popular herbal remedy.

I saw it spreading over a deserted pueblo in New Mexico in the blazing sun, on the dryest of soils.

—HELEN MORGENTHAU FOX

* * *

Certain familiar herbs were not planted in gardens, but only domesticated in and about old farms. . . . This was done with a common herb of country medicine, the old white horehound, that wan, nettle-like presence with its pointed, hostile bracts. . . . To this day, patches of horehound stand back of many old houses on Cape Cod; I often used to come upon them.

—HENRY BESTON

* * *

Horehound. Blossom white. By roadsides and among rubbish. Dr. Withering observes that it was . . . the principal ingredient in Negro Caesar's remedy for vegetable poisons.

—REV. MANASSEH CUTLER

* * *

Today I made horehound candy. . . . Since the first century it has been a valued remedy for coughs. An ancient herbalist once wrote of horehound, "It is bitter to the taste, yet its scent is sweet", and goes on to advise one to "drink horehound if you are poisoned by your stepmother." I wonder if this ancient was drawing upon personal experience.

—ANNIE BURNHAM CARTER

* * *

Elizabethan lady
    In farthingale of leaves,
Stiff ruffs and cuffs of blossom
    And downy velvet sleeves,
Let horehound sit for moonlight
    To songs no longer sung.
I almost taste its flavor
    Half-bitter on my tongue.
              —ELISABETH W. MORSS,
        "Horehound"

IRIS

Iris germanica, I. pallida, I. versicolor; Iridaceae

"Purity, valor, faith, wisdom"

Iris has a long history of symbolism. Named in honor of the Goddess of Rainbows, these charming flowers do indeed display a variety of colors in the flower garden. In the symbolism of heraldry, the Iris ("Fleur de Lys") means faith, wisdom, and valor. It shares with the lily an early Christian symbolism denoting purity and the Virgin Mary. Ancient Egyptians considered Iris to be a symbol of power. In Japan, Iris in an arrangement is said to have a meaning of manly valor. As an herb, it is used principally now as the source for orris root, a valuable powdered fixative in potpourris. Iris germanica and Iris pallida are the types grown in Europe for the use of their roots in the fixative and in perfumery. An American counterpart called Wild Blue Flag (I. versicolor) was used by the Indians in various medicinal remedies. Dwarf varieties of Iris are especially charming in herb gardens, small bouquets, and tussie-mussies.

In this pond the blue flag (*I. versicolor*) grows thinly in the pure water, rising from the stony bottom all around the shore, where it is visited by hummingbirds in June.

—HENRY DAVID THOREAU

* * *

The fresh root [of *I. germanica*] is dug, peeled and sun-dried, then stored for two years to develop the scent. It is then ground and emits the

82

violet odor for which it is known. Orris root is the most common fixative for potpourri as it is easily obtainable. I use it generously, at least 1 cup to 1 pound of rose petals, along with spices and other essences.

—ADELMA G. SIMMONS

IVY

Hedera helix; Araliaceae

"Patience, immortality, fidelity, undying affection, friendship, marriage"

The common ivy is an herb rich in folklore, symbolism, and use. Dedicated to Bacchus, it was once shunned by Christians, but later was used in homes and churches for decorating. Its use in medicine went into an early decline. Although often associated with death and immortality, Ivy's evergreen leaves and clinging habits have also given it an abundant symbolism of eternal life, patience, fidelity, and undying affection. In olden days, Ivy was thought of as a kindly plant, a feminine life-symbol. When used with holly, it brought fertility to a household and was useful as a charm against witches. Ivy has long been used for ornamental effects in gardens, on walls, in flower arrangements, garlands, wreaths, architectural details, and in a Basket of Herbs.

Ivy grows luxuriously in Galilee and on the tablelands of Palestine east of the Jordan. It is an emblem of fidelity. A wreath of ivy was always presented to a newly married couple by priests in classic Greece.

—HESTER METTLER CRAWFORD

* * *

Ivy was a symbol of constancy from its habit of clinging to old ruins of buildings long after they had been abandoned by people. The thought of the constancy of ivy has been embodied in the story of Tristram and Iseult—the tragic lovers unhappily parted by death but buried side by side. Over each grave a plant of ivy began to grow and continued toward the other until the vines became entwined. So the two lovers were again united by the constancy of the ivy.

—ROSETTA E. CLARKSON

LADY'S MANTLE

Alchemilla vulgaris; Rosaceae

"Comfort, protection"

The leaves of Lady's Mantle resemble the pleated folds of a cape that might have protected the Virgin Mary, giving this delightful herb its most popular name and its symbolisms. Other old names for the plant are Lion's Foot, Bear's Foot, and Nine Hooks. In flower arrangements and tussie-mussies, the leaves are effective; the softly yellow blossoms are long lasting and delicate. They also dry well. Once used in medicine, the herb is now principally enjoyed for its beauty in garden and bouquet.

In our herb gardens, Lady's Mantle gives us another exquisite plant in shades of yellow-green. This is a plant which has inspired beautiful designs in painting, botanical illustrations, embroidery, and tapestry. As we contemplate it on a warm sunny day, we see yet another form and pattern for our enjoyment.

—HESTER METTLER CRAWFORD

* * *

[An] herb that retains its dew-studded appearance until high noon is Lady's Mantle. Its ornamental value is in its pleated, fan-shaped leaves of characteristic chartreuse, although they can be a deeper green in some soils. It is displayed to perfection when planted in drifts along the border, either in partial shade or full sun, on a bank or in a rock garden. The . . . small, airy, flowers—also chartreuse—are long lasting and can be dried for winter bouquets.

—PRISCILLA SAWYER LORD

LAVENDER

Lavandula angustifolia; Labiatae

"Constancy, devotion, luck, housewifely virtue, undying love"

A long list of virtuous symbols belongs to Lavender. To many of its devotees it symbolizes grandmothers and their scented linens, sweetly aromatic garden walks, old-fashioned flower borders, and pretty green bottles wrapped in woven straw, containing the Lavender toilet water so indispensable to the 19th-century dressing table. It has long been used for its clean scent in soaps, perfumes, potpourris, and sweet bags. In the garden, the grey-green plants of Lavender with their purple flowers are beloved by bees and visitors, as well as by the gardeners. Lavender is one of the most popular herbs for home and garden, for its fragrant language speaks of cleanness, freshness, beauty, and charm, in addition to all its Victorian symbols and virtues. Truly, Lavender is a flower for every Basket of Herbs.

> Lavender grey, lavender blue
> Perfume wrapt in the sky's own hue.
> —ANONYMOUS

* * *

There will always be a thought of its tall spikes against the whitewashed walls of cottages, and of Lavender walks leading from the kitchen garden to the flowers . . . the most feminine of all herbs. A great favourite in eighteenth century France, when taste and fashion were of feminine inspiration, it was often included in the flower paintings of the time for the

LAVENDER

sake of its leaves flushed purple under green and the French violet of the flowers.

—HENRY BESTON

* * *

[From an 18th-century family receipt book:]

To make a Lavender Sack: Take a basket of lavender flowers, not full blown. Strip the flowers from the stalks. Dry them in the air but not in the sun. Add some of the dried leaves of the plant. Pack them all in a little sack of fine silk or muslin, very closely stuffed. You may put them under your pillows for sleep, and with your linens for perfume.

—PRISCILLA SAWYER LORD

The young year sets the buds astir,
The old year strips the trees;
But ever in my lavender
I hear the brawling bees.
—LIZETTE WOODWORTH REESE,
from "That Day You Came"

* * *

Vinegar of the Four Thieves: Take lavender, rosemary, sage, worm-wood, rue, and mint, of each a handful; put them in a pot of earthenware, pour on them four quarts of very strong vinegar, cover the pot closely, and put a board on the top; keep it in the hottest sun two weeks, then strain and bottle it, putting in each bottle a clove of garlic. When it is settled in the bottle and become clear, pour it off gently; do this until you get it all free from sediment. The proper time to make it is when the herbs are in full vigour, in June. This vinegar is very refreshing in crowded rooms, in the apartments of the sick; and is peculiarly grateful when sprinkled about the house in damp weather.

—MRS. MARY RANDOLPH

LILY OF THE VALLEY

Convallaria majalis; Liliaceae

*"Contentment, return of happiness, purity,
constancy, simplicity; 'Let us make up' "*

The Lily of the Valley is worthy of all the affectionate names it has been given for centuries: May Lily, Mary's Tears, Our Lady's Tears, Jacob's Ladder, Ladder-to-Heaven, Constancy Lily, Flower of Spring, and Whitsuntide Flower. Its list of sentimental meanings is also long and deserved. One of the first flowers of springtime, it is often gathered by children in handsful for a fragrant present to someone they love, and to put into May baskets. No longer used in medicine as in times past, the Lily of the Valley is now an herb to be enjoyed in perfumes, gardens, and bouquets.

> The pushcarts, on the first of May,
> Bring valley-lilies' creamy bells.
> There's luck in sprigs of fresh muguet
> From pushcarts, on the first of May.
> —PAUL SCOTT MOWRER,
> from "The Pushcarts of Paris"

* * *

Since the lily of the valley is one of the first flowers of the year, it has come to signify the coming of spring and summer. In this aspect it appears in Christian tradition as a sign of the advent of Christ in his second coming, for the Last Judgment.

—ANTHONY S. MERCATANTE

There was always a bed of lilies of the valley where nothing else would grow.

—HELEN MCNAUGHTON

* * *

Sweetest of the flowers a-blooming
   In the fragrant vernal days
Is the Lily of the Valley
   With its soft retiring ways.

Well, you chose this humble blossom
   As the nurse's emblem flower,
Who grows more like her ideal
   Every day and every hour.

Like the Lily of the Valley
   In her honesty and worth,
Ah, she blooms in truth and virtue
   In the quiet nooks of earth.

—PAUL LAURENCE DUNBAR,
from "The Lily of the Valley"

MARJORAM – SWEET MARJORAM

Origanum Majorana; Labiatae

"Joy, happiness, kindness"

This favorite plant of all herb lovers is but one of a distinguished family that includes Oregano, wild or pot Marjoram, and Dittany of Crete. One of the most pleasantly scented and flavored herbs to grow, it is allied with human history through the ages. Marjoram has been known in America since the colonists brought seeds with them to their new land as early as 1640. It has always meant joy and happiness in sentimental, garden, and household use. The Greeks and Romans wove wreaths and garlands containing Marjoram for weddings and funerals; it was a strewing herb, a furniture polish, a dye herb and a medicinal herb. Bees find it enchanting; so do the fairies. A sprig of Sweet Marjoram belongs in every potpourri, tussie-mussie, turkey stuffing, green salad or soup, and many other good and useful things. Its blossoms add interest and meaning to a basket of Herbs.

The drifts and patches of wild marjoram in our garden are ever alive with winged creatures—bees, butterflies and an occasional hummingbird, for it offers nectar long after the thymes and lavender have faded.

—PRISCILLA SAWYER LORD

* * *

In the early Greek and Roman days sweet marjoram was used to crown young married couples. It was called the symbol of honor and also was said

93

to possess the gift of banishing sadness. I'm sure that was true because no one could inhale its fragrance without pleasure, or touch its soft velvety leaves without being comforted.

—HELEN S. STEPHENS

* * *

The rosemary and the origan [*sic*] — are they for flavoring the sauce? . . . Of course they're marvellous in other things, soups and dressings for fowls. Herbs get me more excited than anything else that grows, I think. I'm enclosing a post-card to make it easy for you to answer whether or not we should put them in the sauce.

—EDNA ST. VINCENT MILLAY

* * *

Few people know how to keep the flavor of sweet marjoram; the best of all herbs for broth and stuffing. It should be gathered in bud or blossom, and dried in a tin-kitchen at a moderate distance from the fire; when dry, it should be immediately rubbed, sifted, and corked up in a bottle carefully.

—MRS. LYDIA MARIA CHILD

* * *

Marjoram—the very name
Is honey on the lips,
A souvenir of summer sun
And European trips.
Renaissance—one thinks of this
And formal garden plots
And then the simply picturesque,
With gardening in pots.

—ELISABETH W. MORSS,
"Sweet Marjoram"

MIGNONETTE

Reseda odorata; Resedaceae

"Your qualities surpass your charms"

Known as an herb of magic and medicinal power as far back as Pliny's era, Mignonette today spells charm and romance. It is said that Mignonette represented hope for a spurned lover who rolled in its leaves and blossoms three times. In one area of Italy, the herb was used to cure many disorders; when used as a poultice, the peasants chanted a charm thought to be especially effective as an accompaniment to the treatment. Today in France, Mignonette is used in the distillation of perfumes. Its blossoms are fragrant in the garden and in a Basket of Herbs.

> The delicate odour of mignonette,
>> The remains of a dead and gone bouquet,
> Is all that tells of a story; yet
>> Could we think of it in a sweeter way?
>>>> —BRET HARTE

* * *

> Great gardens have a glory though it does not come my way.
> The lure of little gardens is a grace for every day.
> In the white radiance of the dawn, the tenderness of dusk,
> There's magic in the mignonette, and witchery in musk.
>>>> —FLORENCE BONE,
>>>>> from "The Dream Garden"

95

[Mignonette was] . . . known as the fragrant weed when introduced into England in 1751. It came to the British Isles through Holland though it is a native of Egypt. It became a favorite for balcony and window boxes. Planted in this manner it developed long trailing habits and perfumed the air about it. The smallest variety is the sweetest and the fragrance is better in a moist bed.

—ADELMA G. SIMMONS

MINT

Spearmint: Mentha spicata

Peppermint: Mentha piperita

Labiatae

"Eternal refreshment, wisdom, virtue,

warmth of feeling, sentiment"

One cannot count the ways in which various members of the prolific Mint family have been used for centuries. In Biblical days Mint was well known. In mediaeval homes, castles, and monasteries, its refreshing fragrance, flavor, and usefulness in medicine made it essential to well-being, and also denoted wisdom and virtue. In modern times, it is one of the best-loved plants of kitchen, garden, field, and brookside. To everyone, Mint means cool refreshment. While Spearmint and Peppermint are the best known members of the family, others have equal uses. Mints are grown in all temperate regions of the world and in addition to other widespread uses, a sprig or two belongs in every fragrant bouquet.

The bees love any and all Mint-flowers to feast upon. Any Mint, apparently, is supposed to keep away ants and mice. I've tried laying branches about, but couldn't be sure—they might have left for several other reasons; if Mint truly does repel them, it's the most charming repellant imaginable.

—KATHERINE BARNES WILLIAMS

June 25, 1805. [Near Great Falls on the Missouri River.] We have been unsuccessful in our attempt to catch fish . . . in this part of the river. Among the vegetable productions we observe . . . great quantities of mint like the peppermint.

—MERIWETHER LEWIS

* * *

What a variety of old garden herbs, mints, etc., are naturalized along an old settled road like this to Boston which the British travelled! and then there is the site, apparently, of an old garden by the tan-yard, where the spearmint grows so rankly. I am intoxicated by the fragrance.

—HENRY DAVID THOREAU

* * *

The weather had convinced Mrs. Todd that it was time to make a supply of cough-drops, and she had been bringing forth herbs from dark and dry hiding-places, until now the pungent dust and odor of them had resolved themselves into one mighty flavor of spearmint that came from a simmering caldron of syrup in the kitchen. . . . The time of gathering herbs was nearly over, but the time of syrups and cordials had begun.

—SARAH ORNE JEWETT

* * *

The Mint tribe is a large one, and as in most big families, there are endearing members, and then there are those characters who push and shove and try to take over your garden. All of them, however, are spicy and interesting; did Shakespeare call them "hot mints"? Not to the naked tongue perhaps, but in an iced drink, cool as green organza.

—JOSEPHINE GRAY

If whiffs of all the Fragrant Herbs
Could have a special tint,
How lovely would the color be
Above a bed of Mint.

—MARGUERITE H. HICKERNELL
AND ELLA W. BREWER

MYRTLE

Myrtus communis; Myrtaceae

"Love, married bliss, weddings"

The common Myrtle, also sometimes called Greek Myrtle, is an enchanting herb, a shrub which must be wintered indoors in the north. As an ornamental plant, it is easily trained into topiary forms. The glossy dark green leaves and starry white fragrant blossoms give it value as a plant "for use and for delight" in any herb garden or bouquet. Myrtle is an ancient herb, known to the gods and considered sacred to Venus and Aphrodite. It is everywhere a symbol of love, joy, and a happy marriage. Often used in wreaths, garlands, and Baskets of Herbs, it has been used also in perfumery.

The true myrtle is a plant of a long and venerable history. In ancient times it was a symbol of sensual love and passion as well as immortality. . . . It was used in many countries in a bride's bouquet or as a wreath for her head, to symbolize harmony and immortality. . . . To an herb collector it is a plant almost without peer. The fragile beauty of those blossoms sprinkled like star-dust over the handsome leaves was indeed a sight to earn it an honored place in my plant window.

—HALE BUMPUS

* * *

Small shrubs of true myrtle are placed in a narrow bed to remind us that myrtle was one of the plants of Palestine . . . a symbol of the highest good, domestic happiness and love. The tree, once dedicated to Venus, was re-dedicated to the Virgin and became a symbol of virginity.

—ADELMA G. SIMMONS

* * *

The myrtle on thy breast or brow
Would lively hope and love avow.

—SARAH JOSEPHA HALE

NASTURTIUM

NASTURTIUM

Tropaeolum majus, T. minus; Tropaeolaceae

"Patriotism, victory in battle"

Although its many-hued bright flowers might signify gaiety and cheer, this much-loved herb has long had a meaning of patriotism and victory in battle. Its botanical name "tropaeolum" means "trophy," and to be sure the leaf resembles a shield, and the flower a helmet, so its relations to battle are easily identified. In Europe, the flower is sometimes called Indian Cress, as it is a member of the cress family with the same spicy bite to its flavor as salad cresses. It came there by way of the Spaniards, who got it from the natives of Peru. Other names for Nasturtium have been Yellow Lark's Heels and Nose-Twister. From its first entrance into our herb world in the 16th century, Nasturtium's leaves and flowers have been used in salads, and its green seeds have been pickled. Nasturtiums were of such value to Thomas Jefferson's household that they were grown in "a bed 10 yd. by 19." They are favorite flowers to use in fragrant bouquets or nosegays and in Baskets of Herbs.

It is thought the flower [Nasturtium] is superior to a radish in flavour, and is eat in salads or without.

—JOHN RANDOLPH

* * *

Nasturtiums, marigolds and sunflowers were the only innocent gold to reach Europe on the floodtide of treasure that poured from the New

World into the old during the years when Spain was looting her American empire with bloody hands. . . . It was a brutal and reckless time, full of the vitality and excitement that ring in the very title of the book which introduced the Nasturtium to Englishmen: "Joyfull newes out of the Newe Founde Worlde." This book, published in London in 1577, was a translation by one "Jhon Frampton, merchaunt" of *"La Historia Medicinal de las Cosas"* by Dr. Monardes of Seville.

—BUCKNER HOLLINGSWORTH

* * *

To Pickle Nasturtiums: Gather the berries when full grown but young, put them in a pot, pour boiling salt and water on, and let them stand three or four days; then drain off the water, and cover them with cold vinegar; add a few blades of mace, and whole grains of black pepper.

—MRS. MARY RANDOLPH

ORANGE

Sweet Orange: Citrus sinensis

Calamondin: C. Citrofortunella mitis

Rutaceae

"Bridal festivity, chastity, purity, generosity"

First recorded in writings of the Arabs, Orange fruits and blossoms have been used in herbal ways for centuries, especially in essences, perfumes, and potpourris, occasionally in medicine, and to represent purity and chastity as well as festivity at weddings. The familiar pomander ball of today, an orange stuck with cloves is reminiscent of the mediaeval pomanders, which were carried or placed among clothes in a chest for their beneficient fragrance. The bridal custom of carrying a bouquet or wreath of Orange blossoms has come to us from the Saracens. Many old cookbooks contain directions for making and using orange flower water, which has been used in cookery and perfumery for a long time. In New Orleans, the best receipts for a famous beverage there will contain a portion of this delicately flavored essence. Small trees of the miniature orange, Calamondin, are useful and decorative today in herb gardens, the fruits utilized for candy and preserving, for tiny dried pomanders, and the sweet-smelling flowered branches for posies.

The orange tree is regarded as a symbol of purity, chastity, and generosity. Thus it is occasionally depicted in paintings of the Virgin Mary. . . .

The white flower is also used to suggest purity, and for this reason orange blossoms are the traditional adornment of brides.

—GEORGE FERGUSON

* * *

The fashion for blossoming plants indoors in winter was not so easily followed in America. . . . There were few greenhouses and in mid-19th century even a conservatory was considered an unusual feature. In the 1840s, Mrs. James Rush, a famous Philadelphia hostess who never did things by halves, had two much-talked-of conservatories, one at either side of her ballroom. . . . Mrs. Rush, it is said, paid the most minute attention to details when planning her balls and suppers, even to the "ribbons for the programmes and the oranges and lemons to be hung on the orange and lemon trees."

—GEORGIANA REYNOLDS SMITH

* * *

Some three days since on their own soil live-sprouting,
Now here their sweetness through my room unfolding,
A bunch of orange buds by mail from Florida.
—WALT WHITMAN,
"Orange Buds by Mail from Florida"

* * *

[From "The Art of Confectionery, 1866":]

EAU DIVINE: Macerate the zests of three limes and four lemons with four ounces of fresh orange-flowers, one ounce of fresh heads of balm, and six ounces of white hoarhound, in seven pints of alcohol, for ten days; distil in the water-bath, and add a syrup made with three pounds of sugar and one quart of distilled water. . . . Steep ten days. (Used for flavoring beverages, cakes, frostings, etc.)

—JOHN HULL BROWN

PANSY or HEARTSEASE

Viola tricolor; Violaceae

"Thoughts, happy thoughts, meditation"

The ancestor of our modern Pansy, still alive and thriving today, the Heartsease or Johnny-Jump-Up, has a connotation of happy thoughts with a long list of humorous and affectionate common names that have helped endear it to every lover of flowers and herb gardens. Among these delightful names are Lady's Delight, Three Faces under a Hood, Tickle My Fancy, Pink of My Joan, Garden-Gate, None So Pretty, Kit Run About, Come and Cuddle Me, Kiss Me, Jump Up and Kiss Me, Meet Her in the Pantry, Kiss Her in the Butt'ry, and Butterfly Violet. The flowers were long known in Europe, and they were first hybridized in England, resulting in many new varieties, including the giant pansies we know today. In herb gardens and posies, it is the Johnny-Jump-Up which is most loved, and a plant that has seeded itself can be given away but must never be thrown away, for it is good luck to receive a plant from a friend, but bad luck to destroy one.

A window-box of pansies
Is such a happy thing.

—ELEANOR FARJEON,
from "Window Boxes"

PANSY

The pansy, or tri-colored violet adorns the fresh chaplets of April and blends its colors with the yellow sheaves of autumn.

—WILSON FLAGG

* * *

Viola tricolor—Pansy; Lady's Delight. The Heart's Ease, or Pansy, is a general favorite, an old acquaintance with every one who has had anything to do with a flower-garden. It begins to open its modest but lively flowers as soon as the snow clears off in the spring, and continues to enliven the garden till the snow comes again.

—JOSEPH BRECK

PARSLEY

Petroselinum crispum; Umbelliferae

"Festivity"

Parsley's ancient symbolism of Festivity has descended through the years to become a use as garnish on platters and plates of food, but happily we have many other reasons to appreciate this versatile herb. Rich in vitamins and minerals, it has been used by good cooks in many delicious ways. Also rich in chlorophyll, Parsley is an efficient breath sweetener. One of its most charming uses is as an edging plant for a garden; another as a lacy green border around the outside of a tussie-mussie. There is no doubt that Parsley is the most widely known and used herb, and it is in fact indispensable in any herb or kitchen garden. The herb has a long and interesting past, from ancient Greece in funeral ceremonies to crowning winners of games with chaplets and wreaths of Parsley. Originally not used for food, it was occasionally used for medicine, particularly in monasteries of the Middle Ages. Parsley is one of the French fines herbes, and plants grow on the window-sills in many kitchens where other herbs are not well known.

A Victorian girl would be careful not to cut a sprig of Parsley, since this would bring bad luck in love, and if she should give away Parsley, it would be giving away her good luck in such matters. To retrieve it, she could not buy or borrow, but must steal the herb—a dilemma for a Victorian young lady.

—ANTHONY S. MERCATANTE

Where you breed Rabbits it may be sown in the fields; Hares & Rabbits being remarkably fond of it, will resort to it from great distances. . . . If intended for the table, the seed should be sown early in spring; if for medicinal purposes or for rabbits . . . about the middle of March in Va. The gardeners have an advantage as to this plant, that the seed goes 9 times to the devil before it comes up, alluding to the length of time it stays in the ground before it germinates.

—JOHN RANDOLPH

* * *

If parsley were as scarce as sturgeon eggs and as rare as truffles, it would conceivably be one of the world's most sought-after herbs. Happily, it is almost as abundant as meadow grass, as taken for granted in most kitchens throughout the world as salt and pepper. On any given day, it is tossed, in one form or another, into countless soups and stews and assorted ragouts.

—CRAIG CLAIBORNE

* * *

Parsley, of the three kinds, the thickest and branchiest is the best, is sown among onions, or in a bed by itself, may be dryed for winter use . . . a pleasurably tasted herb, and much used in garnishing viands . . . good in soups, and to garnish roast Beef, excellent with bread and butter in the spring.

—AMELIA SIMMONS

The modern use of parsley
Is to place her rather sparsely
As an ornament, for any kind of food.
But when the Ancients found her
With violets they bound her
And wore her to their banquets as a snood.
She makes a charming frilly hedge
And neatly trims the border's edge.

—L. YOUNG CORRETHERS,
from "Parsley"

PENNYROYAL

Mentha Pulegium; Labiatae

"Protection; 'Flee away'"

Often found in cottage gardens and fields of Old and New England, Pennyroyal was deemed a remedy for many common ills, and Pennyroyal tea was one of the substitutes for China tea in colonial America. English Pennyroyal has in common with our native American plant a strong, pungent, minty cool fragrance. The Pennyroyals bore many country names, such as Run-by-the-Ground, Lurk-in-the-Ditch, Pudding Grass, Tick Weed, Squaw Mint, and Flea-Away. It has been a traditional herb for the crib in Christmas nativity scenes, as it was once believed that Pennyroyal would burst into bloom at midnight on Christmas Eve. Rubbed on the face, neck, and ankles while gardening, Pennyroyal is said to make mosquitoes and black flies vanish, an attribute which by itself tempts a gardener to grow it lavishly.

Pennyroyal is found in dry places from Canada southward through New England. It is usually in the company of meadow violets, wild strawberries and black-eyed susans.

—GERTRUDE B. FOSTER,
Herbs for Every Garden

* * *

Penny Royal is a high aromatic, altho a spontaneous herb in old ploughed fields, yet might be more generally cultivated in gardens and used in cookery and medicines.

—AMELIA SIMMONS

I pluck dry sprigs of pennyroyal which I love to put in my pocket, for it scents me thoroughly and reminds me of garrets full of herbs. . . . How often I have found pennyroyal by the fragrance it emitted when bruised by my feet! . . . . We were most interested to hear of the pennyroyal; it is soothing to be reminded that wild nature produces anything ready for the use of man.

—HENRY DAVID THOREAU

* * *

This herb has been continuously used by our people. It was one of the most cherished herbs of Colonial days, a "hanging herb," always found in quantities in attics for medicinal use. Any walk through the woods or countryside is more comfortable if a bunch of Pennyroyal is carried or the plant crushed and rubbed on legs and arms.

—SIDNEY DUERR

* * *

. . . [W]e set forward in a narrow footpath and made our way to a lonely place that faced northward, where there was more pasturage and fewer bushes, and we went down to the edge of short grass above some rocky cliffs where the deep sea broke with a great noise, though the wind was down and the water looked quiet a little way from shore. Among the grass grew such pennyroyal as the rest of the world could not provide. There was a fine fragrance in the air as we gathered it sprig by sprig and stepped along carefully, and Mrs. Todd pressed her aromatic nosegay between her hands and offered it to me again and again.

"There's nothin' like it," she said; "oh no, there's no such pennyr'yal as this in the State of Maine. It's the right pattern of the plant, and all the rest I ever see is but an imitation. Don't it do you good?" And I answered with enthusiasm.

—SARAH ORNE JEWETT

'Twas pennyroyal bloomed that night
The angels came to earth
And o'er the stall at Bethlehem
Proclaimed our Saviour's birth.

—ANONYMOUS

PINKS

Dianthus Caryophyllus; Caryophyllaceae

Pink, Carnation: "Resignation, pure love"

Clove Pink: "Lasting beauty, affection"

Old-fashioned clove pinks are not found often enough in herb gardens of today, for in addition to their herbal history, they have a sweet fragrance that is valuable in potpourris and nosegays. Clove pinks sometimes performed as informal borders in our grandmothers' gardens. They were called Clove Gilliflowers, Ruffling Robins, July Flowers, or Carnations. One of the popular old names, Sops in Wine, denotes an early use as flavoring for wine, which was served especially at Christmas. An Arab receipt for Ratafia called for "striped pinks," spirits, juice of strawberries, and saffron. The flowers were sometimes used to make vinegar, cordials, syrups, and conserves, as well as perfumes. In America, the flower was listed in Prince's catalog in 1790, and Bartram carried it in 1814. Fragrant Pink flowers were once used in chaplets and crowns. Hybridizing of the beloved flower was a popular pastime for Elizabethan gardeners, resulting in many types and colors of the Carnation. So rare is the old-fashioned Pink, Clove Gilliflower, that it is now rather difficult to find the seed or a cutting, but the ancient charm and spicy scent are worth the search.

Dianthus, signifying the Flower of God, or divine flower; so named on account of its preeminent beauty. Most of the species of this genus are highly valued, not only for the beauty of their flower but also as being evergreen; their foliage during winter, being as abundant and as vivid as in summer. The fragrance of some of the species is peculiarly grateful, and no plant in this respect surpasses the Clove Pink.

—JOSEPH BRECK

* * *

The old-fashioned single country Pink . . . was often used as an edging for small borders, and its bluish green, almost gray, foliage was quaint in effect and beautiful in the moonlight. . . . The scent was wafted down the garden path and along the country road. . . . A garden childhood gives more sources of delight to the senses in after life that come from beautiful color and fine fragrance. . . . The Clove Carnation is the best of all. It feels just as it smells.

—ALICE MORSE EARLE

POPPY

Papaver (P. somniferum); Papaveraceae

"Sleep, oblivion, fertility, extravagance, ignorance, consolation, sadness"

As varied as are the kinds and colors of Poppies grown in gardens are their uses: ornamental in the borders, brilliantly cheerful naturalized in the fields and on hillsides, hypnotic and sedative in medicine, and deliciously sharp when seeds are used in breads and cakes. In addition to their ancient symbolisms, we now value Poppies for their beauty, and for seeds to use in the kitchen. The petals of some Poppies have been used as a dye and to make ink; the dried seed pods are useful in flower arrangements.

Scattering Poppy seeds on bread and cakes is so old a custom that the directions for making the seeds stick are found in Pliny.

—HELEN MORGENTHAU FOX

* * *

My garden and my flowers have never been so lovely in spite of the dry weather. A new feature is the Shirley Poppies from white through every heavenly shade and tint of rose, to the most radiant and delicate scarlet glory—wonderful. I pile them in a pyramid on the bookcase opposite the windows in graduated shades and they are like a rosy dawn, Aurora herself.

—CELIA THAXTER

* * *

The opium poppy is not a native of the Far East but rather of the Mediterranean area. Its remains have been found in prehistoric Swiss lake-

village ruins and it grew widely from North Africa through the Levant.
. . . Even Gerard noted garden varieties available in 1597.

—EDGAR ANDERSON

* * *

The harvesting of the poppy crop, in oriental countries, especially in
India, has the appearance of a wholesome family enterprise, and there is
enough beauty in its rhythmic ritual to form a theme for a lovely ballet.

—DOROTHY BOVÉE JONES,
The Herbarist 1958

ROSE

ROSE

Rosa; Rosaceae

"Love, victory, pride"

Geological traces of the earliest American Roses have been found etched by the ages into rocks in the remotest Rocky Mountains of Colorado and Oregon, and Roses seem to have grown in temperate climates all over the world forever. William Penn, returning in 1699 from England to the colonies, brought back eighteen Rose bushes. Washington and Jefferson prized them in their gardens, and the history of the Rose on the grounds of the White House began in 1800, when practical John Adams planted a combined Rose and kitchen garden. It is not only their incomparable beauty, but their ancient association with man and his loves, that endear the Rose to every gardener. In universal legend and myth, medicine and perfumery, politics and war, religion, literature and art, in song and dance and play, in kitchen and stillroom and parlor as well as garden, the Rose has found a place. A pink Rose in the center of a bunch of scented violets is the world's sweetest nosegay.

Why should a rose be an herb? . . . . Since prehistory they have been employed as curatives for various ills, as condiments in foods, and for healthful and soothing drinks. The origins and birthplace of roses are uncertain, but their history is very old . . . they have existed in the United States for at least thirty-two million years.

—MARGARET E. PINNEY

The rose is a rose,
    And was always a rose.
But the theory now goes
    That the apple's a rose,
And the pear is, and so's
    The plum, I suppose.
The dear only knows
    What will next prove a rose.
You, of course, are a rose—
    But were always a rose.

                —ROBERT FROST,
             "The Rose Family"

* * *

The Cherokee Indians regard all flowers as friendly beings whose beauty
is a reflection of love and whose petals bring healing. The white blossoms
known as the Cherokee Rose had for them an additional message. It tells
Indians to remain together under the pine fringes of the forest, and that
no white man can inflict in them a sorrow that cannot be borne with patience and dignity. . . . Often called white brier roses, they are the only
flowers that the young braves gather for their brides to garland their raven
hair. The maiden who wears these flowers will live happily and securely
with her chosen love.

                —JEAN GORDON

* * *

. . . [G]ardens in the South were filled with charming old-fashioned
roses with pleasant names and delightful perfume. Unchecked by the
pruning shears, they grew to ample proportions and bloomed generously
from spring to fall.

                —ELIZABETH LAWRENCE

Why does the painful thorn presume
To spoil the Rose's soft perfume?
It was by Providence intended
Our pains and pleasures should be blended;

We smile today, tomorrow mourn
Nor find a rose without a thorn.

—MISS FITTON

* * *

The birds scattered the seed everywhere and the rugosa rose took root all along the Marblehead coast and, by the same process, elsewhere along the entire seaboard. The brilliant red fruits or hips . . . are a prime source of concentrated Vitamin C. Both the wild "damask" and the rugosa rose send forth a few blooms even into late November, and no bit of living color is more welcome at this time of year.

—PRISCILLA SAWYER LORD

* * *

. . . On one side of the portal, and rooted almost at the threshold, was a wild rose bush, covered, in this month of June, with its delicate gems, which might be imagined to offer their fragrance and fragile beauty to the prisoner. . . . Finding it so directly on the threshold of our narrative, which is now about to issue from that inauspicious portal, we could hardly do otherwise than pluck one of its flowers and present it to the reader. It may serve, let us hope, to symbolize some sweet moral blossom, that may be found along the track, or relieve the darkening close of a tale of human frailty and sorrow.

—NATHANIEL HAWTHORNE, of the rose growing beside the door of the jail in which Hester Prynne was imprisoned.

I never wanted to be a bug
Until I found one safe and snug
In the velvet heart of a pale pink rose
With petals tucked about his toes.
                    —MARION LEE,
                        "Lap of Luxury"

ROSEMARY

Rosmarinus officinalis; Labiatae

"Remembrance, love, loyalty; 'Your presence revives me'"

Rosemary has a very special place in the hearts of herb gardeners for its fragrance and flavor, and for its symbolism of remembrance. Names for this beloved herb include the translation of its Latin name "Rosmarinus," "Dew of the Sea"; also "Coronarius," because it was used to crown the heads of young people in Roman festivals; Rosemarine, which was Shenstone's spelling in "The Schoolmistress," 1735; and Rosemarie, an old popular usage. While Rosemary has long meant Remembrance and was believed to strengthen the memory when consumed, its special message in a Victorian gift of flowers was "Your presence revives me." A sprig of Rosemary was a symbol also of constancy, fidelity, and loyalty; it indicated enduring love and devotion, the holy, the bridal, and the magical. Long ago it was thought to protect against evil spirits, lightning, and injury, to be a favored herb of the fairies, to bring success, and to effect a love charm. A sprig in a letter still becomes a token of love, friendship and remembrance.

Across the world, wherever it grows, a sprig of Rosemary is never just a fragrant green herb, but a bit of human history in one's hands.

—DOROTHY BOVÉE JONES,
The Herbarist 1961

ROSEMARY

A sprig of Rosemary I give
To speak of all the past . . .
—NAN DANE

* * *

Alcoholic perfumes are supposed to have been first made in the four-teenth century, and the first of these of which we have an account is Hungary water, distilled from Rosemary in thirteen hundred and seventy, by Elizabeth, Queen of Hungary, who obtained the recipe from a hermit, and by its use is said to have preserved her beauty to old age.
—CHARLES E. HAMLIN

* * *

Unspoiled of April's rain, by August's fire,
  And incorrupt before October's gold,
Green in December's snows—such I desire
  To be the memory of good friends of old:
Unchanged, unfearing, fragrant, as the semblance
Of Rosemary in my heart's garden of remembrance.
—GEORGE P. BAKER

* * *

Used at weddings, Rosemary was either gilded or dipped in scented water and carried in the Bride's wreath. It silently bade the bride bear away to her new home the remembrance of the dear old roof tree which had sheltered her youth and the loving hearts which had cherished her.
—HELEN NOYES WEBSTER

* * *

Beauty and Beauty's son and rosemary—
Venus and Love, her son, to speak plainly—
born of the sea supposedly,

at Christmas each, in company,
braids a garland of festivity.
 Not always rosemary—
since the flight to Egypt, blooming differently.
With lancelike leaf, green but silver underneath,
its flowers—white originally—
turned blue. The herb of memory,
imitating the blue robe of Mary,
 is not too legendary

to flower both as symbol and as pungency.
the height of Christ when thirty-three—
Springing from stones beside the sea,
not higher—it feeds on dew and to the bee
"hath a dumb language"; is in reality
 a kind of Christmas-tree.

—MARIANNE MOORE,
from "Rosemary"

RUE

Ruta graveolens; Rutaceae

"Sorrow, grace, clear vision, disdain"

A favorite herb of Elizabethan poets and apothecaries, Rue was known as "The Herb of Grace," for branches were once used to sprinkle holy water over the heads of sinners to cleanse them. Rue may also mean regret and repentance; pity and mercy; magic and witchcraft. It occasionally makes known its mystical powers by producing a rash when its leaves are bruised. Old beliefs held that Rue possessed an ability to bestow second sight, and that a sprig laid over the door kept any witch away. An herb with an ancient history of ritual and legendry as well as protection from disease, Rue is essential for a "magic" wreath or bouquet.

> Rue and roses; is it so,
> Where roses blossom, must rue grow,
> And shade the roses, as they blow?
>
> So long as love and sorrow meet,
> So long must rue and roses sweet
> Together bloom to be complete.
> —CAROLINE HAZARD,
> from "Rue and Roses"

Were it ever to come to pass that I could have but two herbs in the garden, Rue would always be the other. . . . Mysterious in colour and strange of leaf, potent, ancient, and dark, Rue is the herb of magic, the symbol of the earthly unknown.

—HENRY BESTON

* * *

For one shall grasp
and one resign,
One drink life's rue,
and one its wine.

—JOHN GREENLEAF WHITTIER (attrib.),
from the pages of a handwritten
Victorian autograph album

SAGE

Salvia officinalis; Labiatae

"Wisdom, long life, immortality, esteem, pity"

Sage is a familiar plant in kitchen and herb garden; and because of the soft grey-green color and texture of its leaves, also provides interest in the flower garden. Its flavor and fragrance give it value in cookery, in scented mixtures and in a comforting tea. Many an old adage alludes to the properties of Sage in healing, prolonging life and giving wisdom. It is known for its charm in attracting bees, for benefiting cheese and ale, and in repelling insects in house and garden. In America, Sage is entwined in Thanksgiving tradition because of its use in the turkey dressing, and at Christmas it has been used to counteract the richness of the festive roast goose. A number of delightful varieties of Sage are of interest to herb gardeners, including those whose plots are limited to a window-sill.

> In snuff and teas and recipes,
>   Sage meant longer life,
> But thumb too green and it could mean
>   Husband ruled by wife.
>   —ELISABETH W. MORSS

* * *

For gaining a Lawful Suit: It reads, if anyone has to settle any just claim by way of a law suit let him take some of the largest kind of sage and write

SAGE

the name of the twelve apostles on the leaves, and put them in his shoes before entering the courthouse, and he shall certainly gain the suit.

—ANNE G. HAYWARD

* * *

All around
Scent of flowers and scent of sage,
Scent of pollen in the pines,
Scent of new-mown grass and clover
Make the morning fragrant.

—EDNA DAVIS ROMIG,
from "The Chickadees"

Every section of our country has native fragrant herbs. In Southern California the sage (Salvia clevelandii) possesses a pungent-scent, reminding one of the out-of-doors. Kitchen sachets [can be] made of Cleveland's Blue Sage with health-giving virtues!

—MAYRE B. RICHARDSON

* * *

The Chinese cannot understand why we import tea from them when we have Sage. They use it with full appreciation of its wonderful value and have been willing to swap with us at a ratio of four to one. In this country sage tea sweetened with maple sugar is a Vermont tradition.

—EDNA CASHMORE

ST. JOHN'S WORT

Hypericum perforatum; Hypericaceae

"Superstition, animosity"

This ancient herb is found growing in field and roadside over many temperate areas of the world today just as it has done for centuries. Its very meanings tell us of its history in folklore. While it once had a reputation as a medicinal herb, it is not so used today. A sprig of its golden blossoms in a nosegay of herbs is sure to keep away all witches, thunderstorms, and evil spirits.

> I have remembered when the winter came . . .
> How in the shimmering noon of summer past
> Come unrecorded beam slanted across
> The upland pastures where the Johnswort grew.
> —HENRY DAVID THOREAU

* * *

All summer the golden-yellow blossoms of the common Saint John's-wort brighten the fields and roadsides. As the Latin name indicates, the leaves, speckled with translucent dots, appear to be perforated. . . . Adventure lovers will be pleased to know that anyone who steps on the plant on Saint John's Eve may expect a little excitement. A magical horse will spring up from the ground beneath the person and carry him away; the excursion, however, ends abruptly at sunrise.

—BARBARA POND

SANTOLINA

Santolina Chamaecyparissus; Compositae

"Wards off evil; 'Many virtues'"

One of the delights of Santolina is to hold one of its small yellow composite flowers in the hand just as the first row of star-like blossoms heralds the opening of the whole flower. Sometimes now called Lavender Cotton, it was once called Ground Cypress by the Romans. A dainty plant, today it is found in herb gardens for its foliage colors of grey or green, its leaf textures and form, its fragrance, and for use in knots and borders. One of the valued herbs early American colonists brought with them to their new home, Santolina was then used as a stimulant or medicine, but is no longer considered of value in these respects. Moths don't appreciate the strong fragrance, but in a potpourri or sweet bag, people enjoy it. Country folk believed a sprig of the plant was useful in keeping evil spirits away.

What the herb suggests more than anything else is a little tree a foot high of silvery green-grey coral.

—HENRY BESTON

* * *

More commonly, the name for it
For reasons I've forgotten,
Is this, which does not seem to fit—
Lavender cotton.

—ELISABETH W. MORSS,
from "Santolina"

Clusters of button-like blooms of deep yellow appear in late June and last well into August. Near the sea it flowers profusely. Since it is a fire-resistant plant, it is recommended around public buildings, especially those built of wood.

—PRISCILLA SAWYER LORD

SAVORY

Summer: Satureja hortensis

Winter: S. montana

Labiatae

"Interest, spiciness"

Savory was a plant of the satyrs, according to mythology, and was used for a long list of ailments, including the sting of a bee or wasp. Long used as a kitchen herb, it is commonly called "the bean herb" because it especially enhances the flavor of beans or peas. John Josselyn mentioned the presence of Savory in the New England area in his New-Englands Rarities, *published in 1672. Aromatic and flavorful, the Savories, both summer and winter varieties, were favorite herbs in America; the early cookbooks spell out their uses. The Savories' sentimental meanings of interest and spiciness undoubtedly came from their culinary properties.*

It is this pleasant annual (Summer Savory) which is the true Satureia, the plant loved of the Satyrs and grown by them in rustic pots. . . . The seed we sow is a little put between our fingers by those half-human and immortal hands.

—HENRY BESTON

* * *

Winter Savory is one of the most decorative plants in the herb garden with its little white florets scattered amongst the bright green leaves as if

it had just begun to snow. . . . Charming as a border and if left undis-
turbed it forms a thick, undulating ribbon and when sheared makes a stiff
little hedge.

—HELEN MORGENTHAU FOX

* * *

We left Tancook Island carrying a large two pound bag of summer
savory. . . . The price was . . . reasonable considering the great quantity of plants required to produce a pound of dried savory, the careful cul-
tivation, and the amount of rubbing. As the ferry carried us back to the
mainland Jean and I felt we had spent a very educational, profitable, and
delightful day on the island of summer savory.

—GEORGE L. WEST

SOAPWORT

Saponaria officinalis; Caryophyllaceae

"Cleanliness"

Beloved by country dwellers of Europe and America for a long time, Soapwort has several sentimental names which describe its uses: Latherwort, Fuller's Herb, Bruisewort, Crow Soap; its most common name, Bouncing Bet, portrays its habit of waving in the summer breezes along the roadside or in the fields. Although in years past the herb was occasionally used in medicinal ways, it is most often thought of as being an efficient soap for delicate materials, for washing linens and tapestries and for cleaning the hands of busy gardeners and housewives. It was also useful in washing the delicate white kid gloves of yesteryear.

Bouncing Bet makes ribbons of pinkish white bloom along the roads for several months in mid-summer. . . . As herbs they have never lost their reputation because today hand-weavers and home-dyers use the suds created by dousing the flower heads in water for washing delicate woolens.

—GERTRUDE B. FOSTER

* * *

New England textile manufacturers cleaned and thickened woolen cloth with bouncing bet in a process called "fulling," accounting for . . . [the] name "fuller's herb."

—BARBARA POND

. . . A dash of pink, a haunting, gentle fragrance,
A patch of grass-grown, lusty Bouncing Bet.

Most loyalist of all capricious flowers
Who strayed from dooryard gardens into space
Who knows what pull of supernatural powers
Have kept you near your old abiding place
To mark—what long-gone joys, what griefs, what tears
Here on this spot, left for a hundred years.

—ELIZABETH THROCKMORTON COOKE

(WILD) STRAWBERRY

(WILD) STRAWBERRY

Fragaria vesca, F. virginiana; Rosaceae

"Perfect righteousness, perfection, foresight, good works"

The American Wild Strawberry is one of the most delightful of herbs and has been appreciated since its discovery by the first European emigrants to our shores for its fragrance, flavor, and usefulness. The Wild Strawberry has many connotations of goodness; it can also signify intoxication, delight, and "You are delicious" in the language of herbs. A whole sprig of Wild Strawberry and its leaves is a gift of good luck to a lady. The leaves alone mean completeness and perfection; the blossoms mean foresight and are sacred to the fairies of the garden. While once used in medicinal ways, we value the Wild Strawberry now principally for the pleasure of eating it, as a motif in arts, and as borders in the herb garden—and perhaps its leaves in tea, as in Revolutionary days, when patriotic housewives gathered and dried them to provide a substitute for China tea.

Captain John Smith, dusting his hands of indigent Virginians and sailing along a rugged coast to name it New England, had forehandedly planted his own little garden for "sallets" on a rocky island on the coast of Maine. Careful observer of the profusion of berries growing upon a bank of the Piscataqua River, he named it "Strawbery Banke." [Note: "Strawbery Banke," in New Hampshire, was renamed "Portsmouth" in 1653.]

—ANN LEIGHTON

Sat. June 12, 1630 . . . most of our people went on shore upon the land of Cape Ann, which lay very near us, and gathered store of fine strawberries.

—JOHN WINTHROP

* * *

[New York] We had not peas or strawberries here till the 8th day of this month. On the same day I heard the first whip-poor-will whistle. . . . When had you peas, strawberries, and whip-poor-will in Virginia? Take notice hereafter whether the whip-poor-will always come with the strawberries and peas.

—THOMAS JEFFERSON,
from a letter to his daughter Maria, at
home in Monticello, June 13, 1790

On the threshold of summer, Nature proffers us this her virgin fruit; more rich and sumptuous are to follow, but the wild delicacy and fillip of the strawberry are never repeated,—that keen feathered edge greets the tongue in nothing else. . . . The strawberry in the main repeats the form of the human heart, and perhaps, of all the small fruits known to man, none other is so deeply and fondly cherished, or hailed with such universal delight, as this lowly but youth-renewing berry.

—JOHN BURROUGHS

* * *

Tomorrow it will be the same:
Cakes and strawberries
And needles in and out of cloth.
—AMY LOWELL,
from "Interlude"

SWEET WOODRUFF

Galium odoratum; Rubiaceae

"Humility"

A *favorite herb in Elizabethan times for garlands, wreaths, tussie-mussies, floor strewings, and to give a sweet woodsy flavor to wine, Sweet Woodruff is planted today where it can spread and become naturalized in shady places in the garden, its fragrance permeating the air. It signifies Humility because it grows shyly close to the ground. In May, Sweet Woodruff is at its best, in bloom, and it is then used in Maywine, or in a Maybowl of punch, to be decorated with tiny sprigs of the herb and fresh strawberries for a festive occasion. It was once thought that consuming Sweet Woodruff would make the heart merry, as no doubt it would, with the addition of the wine. Sweet Woodruff can be used as a fixative in potpourris and snuff as well as in perfumes and a Basket of Herbs, fresh or dried.*

Today I have walked far, and at the end of my walk I found the little white-flowered Woodruff. It grew in a copse of young ash.

—GEORGE GISSING

* * *

Bunches of Woodruff hung up to dry will fill a whole attic with a fragrance like new-mown hay, and dried and seasoned will make an interesting brew often used by gypsies as a tea.

—HENRY BESTON

Sweet woodruff is an ideal ground cover for shady places. It is a gem of a plant in every respect, with neat whorls of lanceolate leaves and sheets of minute white star-shaped blossoms in spring. Sweet woodruff is one of the herbs valued by flower arrangers who enjoy using distinctive foliage. A cutting or two . . . in an arrangement is reputed to help keep the water fresh.

—PRISCILLA SAWYER LORD

TANSY

Tanacetum vulgare

(T. vulgare var. crispum—Fern-Leafed Tansy)

Compositae

"Hostile thoughts, immortality"

Tansy's traditional meaning of hostility must surely come from its sharp acrid odor. Ages ago this herb was used as a strewing herb and also as an embalming agent for its symbolism of immortality and its long-lasting qualities. It has a history of usefulness in medicine, but today is valued for its beauty in garden and fields, as a natural dye, and by adventuresome cooks as an ingredient of puddings and omelets as of long ago. Many early American housewives rubbed Tansy leaves on their kitchen tables, or grew it at the kitchen door, to keep flies and ants away. Occasionally Tansy has been called Scented Fern, Cow Bitters, Button Bitters, Golden Buttons, and, less charmingly, Stinking Willie. It may have been one of the Biblical bitter herbs of Passover. At Easter time it has been a custom to use Tansy as a flavoring in cakes, omelets or scrambled eggs.

Some old flowers adapt themselves to modern conditions and look up-to-date; but to me the Tansy, wherever found, is as openly old-fashioned as a betty-lamp or a foot-stove.

—ALICE MORSE EARLE

148

A bit of tansy's pungency and I am a little girl trudging along a narrow dusty path in New Jersey where tansy had become naturalized . . . touch but an herb and release a memory.

—MIRA CULIN SAUNDERS

* * *

. . . [S]he explained that there was no tansy in the neighborhood with such snap to it as some that grew about the schoolhouse lot. Being scuffed down all the spring made it grow so much the better, like some folks that had it hard in their youth and were bound to make the most of themselves before they died.

—SARAH ORNE JEWETT

* * *

It may be, when my heart is dull,
    Having attained its girth,
I shall not find so beautiful
    The meager shapes of earth.
Nor linger in the rain to mark
The smell of tansy through the dark.

—EDNA ST. VINCENT MILLAY

* * *

Aside from many other things, spring . . . means that a few families at least enjoy tansy pudding, a confection made from the juice of the fresh young feathery shoots of the tansy plant. Tansy is a pungent, weedy herb that sports little yellow button-like flowers in terminal clusters in summer. This wayside plant was once cultivated in colonial gardens and used for a tonic and as a panacea for various ailments.

—PRISCILLA SAWYER LORD

THYME

THYME

Thymus praecox ssp. articus (Mother-of-Thyme),

T. vulgaris, (garden or common Thyme); Labiatae

Labiatae

"Activity, bravery, courage, strength"

Many varieties of this ancient herb are treasured today for their color and texture, fragrance and flavor, their usefulness in the home, and their traditional symbolisms. Long before it became one of the basic seasonings in French cookery as one of the fines herbes, *it was valued by the Greeks and Romans as flavoring for cheese and liqueurs, for its cleansing and healing qualities in medicine. It is one of the herbs still used today in pharmaceutical ways. Bees have a great affection for beds of Thyme, as do herb gardeners in many countries of the world. In cookery, it is an indispensable but strong herb, proving that good things often come in small packages. No herb garden, spice shelf, or Basket of Herbs is complete without its Thyme.*

The Thymes are herbs of the classical world, plants of the old agriculture and the gods, the proverbial bee-pasture of husbandry and poetry, the symbol of things cherished and of honeyed and fragrant sweetness. Where they grow, the shadows which enclose the old classical imagery always seem to lift a little, allowing us to see again the farmhouse with its Roman tiles, the spring clearer than crystal, and Soracte white with snow. . . . A plant of Thyme in flower is a delight in the garden.

—HENRY BESTON

These herbs are more than just aromatic plants for the garden; they are combined fragrances of sweet lore and legend from ancient times. It used to be the custom for maidens to wear a nose-gay of sprigs of Thyme, Mint and Lavender to bring them sweethearts. Perhaps from your garden will go forth many a little cluster of these herbs, borne in high hopes by feminine visitors.

—ROSETTA E. CLARKSON

* * *

In the foothills of the Catskills, in New York State, there is a tract of acres and acres of rolling country, tinged at its season with the rich purple of wild Thyme . . . the story is that the seed was brought to this country years ago in the wool of imported sheep who had grazed on Grecian hillsides. From this small beginning the plants with their natural ability grew and spread, and many visitors go yearly to see the purple acres and taste the honey.

—ANONYMOUS,
The Herbarist 1956

* * *

At Stockbridge [Massachusetts] the old cemetery is almost entirely covered with thyme of very old growth. It is kept mown and grows with the density of moss, making a springy carpet which releases fragrance as you walk. This is a shady spot, but it does well. As we motored down toward Connecticut later, there were great patches of thyme colonized along the roadside.

—ANONYMOUS,
The Herbarist 1950

And oh ye high flown quills
   that soar the skies,
And ever with your prey still
   catch your praise,
If e'er you deign these lowly
   lines your eyes,
Give thyme or parsley wreath,
   I ask no bays;
This mean and unrefined ore of
   mine
Will make your glist'ring gold
   but more to shine.

—ANNE BRADSTREET

If Mrs. Todd had occasion to step into the far corner of her herb plot, she trod heavily upon thyme, and made its fragrant presence known with all the rest. Being a very large person, her full skirts brushed and bent almost every slender stalk that her feet missed. You could always tell when she was stepping about there, even when you were half awake in the morning, and learned to know, in the course of a few weeks' experience, in exactly which corner of the garden she might be.

—SARAH ORNE JEWETT

* * *

The little low and creeping thymes now comfortably
    sprawl
Upon the crevices stepping stones beyond the
    sheltering wall,
Sun-warmed, mist-laved, brushed by the southwest
    breeze . . .

—GLADYS JENKINS,
    from "The Little Creeping Thymes"

* * *

ABOUT THYME

An herb that's superb
If curbed when served.

—DEBORAH WEBSTER GREELEY

VERBENA (Lemon)

Aloysia triphylla; Verbenaceae

"Delicacy of feeling, enchantment"

Lemon verbena is known and loved by all gardeners who plant flowers for their fragrance, and by all tea-drinkers who appreciate the steeped fragrance and flavor in the delicate leaves. Of great value for its sweet-smelling attributes, it is used in perfumes, potpourris, scent bags, flower arrangements, finger-bowls, and nosegays. Sometimes also called Vervain and Herb Louisa, Verbena was once believed to be an enchanters' herb, protecting its wearer from all evil. In a painting of Mrs. Benjamin Rush by Charles Willson Peale (now at the Boston Museum of Fine Arts), a sprig of Lemon Verbena adorns her bodice, said to have been a device of the artist to remind him of the perfume his subject was wearing. In warm climates of the temperate zones, Lemon Verbena will grow to a large size, becoming a shrub or shrubby tree, but in cold climates it requires a winter home indoors.

Pots filled with lemon verbena standing on the terrace of the porch where we drink tea or after-dinner coffee give off their pleasant perfume as we walk past them and our clothes or hands touch their leaves.

—HELEN MORGENTHAU FOX

LEMON VERBENA

If I were allowed only to grow
One fragrant herb, I know
I would choose Lemon Verbena.
Oh Yes! my views are prejudiced
I'll admit it's so.
But I love the way she scents my garden;
At close of day
On a silver plate
In a crystal bowl
A spray of her leaves
Delights my soul.

—L. YOUNG CORRETHERS

* * *

Even you, Sweet Basil: even you,
Lemon verbena: must exert yourselves now and
　　somewhat harden
Against untimely frost; I have hovered you and
　　covered you and kept going smudges,
Until I am close to worn-out. Now, you
Go about it. I have other things to do,
Writing poetry, for instance. And I, too,
Live in this garden.

—EDNA ST. VINCENT MILLAY,
from "Steepletop"

VIOLET

Viola odorata; Violaceae

"Humility, modesty, devotion, faithfulness"

An extensive family indeed, today's violets may all have sprung from the Sweet Violet, which grows wild in many parts of the temperate zones. With heart-shaped leaves and sweet scent, they live up to their symbolisms. Beloved of bee and butterfly, nature- and flower-lover, child and plant collector, violets are also beloved of herbarists, who use them copiously for their perfume and their beauty in potpourri and nosegay, in candied sweets, syrups, and salads, and for decorating festive cakes and cookies. A May basket filled with violets is an old-fashioned love token fondly remembered.

I have seen a bunch of violets in a glass vase, tied loosely with a straw, which reminded me of myself. —

> I am a parcel of vain strivings tied
> By a chance bond together,
> Dangling this way and that, their links
> Were made so loose and wide,
> Methinks,
> For milder weather.

A bunch of violets without their roots,
And sorrel intermixed,
Encircled by a wisp of straw
Once coiled about their shoots,
The law
By which I'm fixed.
—HENRY DAVID THOREAU

* * *

In the New England countryside, May Day is . . . the arrival of real spring. The early morning mist rises with the sun over the east field, curling like smoke to disappear into the trees and the warming blue sky. Bees buzz in full-blown orchards. There is a spreading of gay color across valleys and hills. Every path we take is embroidered in flowers: violets and spring beauty and the sweet Mayflower.
—MARY MASON CAMPBELL

* * *

A health unto the happy,
A fig for him who frets!
It isn't raining rain to me,
It's raining violets.
—ROBERT LOVEMAN

* * *

Every year, on the day when Laura found the first violet, her mother made a layer cake, and an upside-down pudding celebrated the return of the first robin.

—ELIZABETH COATSWORTH

Belated wanderer of the ways of spring,
Lost in the chill of grim November rain,
Would I could read the message that you bring
And find in it the antidote for pain.

—PAUL LAWRENCE DUNBAR,
from "To a Violet Found
on All Saints Day"

* * *

Who bends a knee where violets grow
A hundred secret things shall know.

—RACHEL FIELD,
from "A Charm of Spring"

YARROW

Achillea millefolium; Compositae

"Health, war"

Once considered a true symbol of war, Yarrow was also thought to be of value for its virtues in providing good health when drunk in an infusion, and for producing visions of future husbands to love-sick girls. There are many old country names listed for this common herb of roadside and field, among them Old Man's Pepper, Soldiers' Woundwort, Thousand Weed, Staunch-Weed (attesting to its medicinal properties), Yarroway, and Devil's Nettle. Although at one time used as a salad green, Yarrow has a bitter taste not often endearing itself to a salad-fancier today. Yarrows' composite flowers of white, occasionally pale lilac, yellow, or deep pink may be dried for flower arrangements; garden varieties make fine accents in garden or bouquet.

As we rode from Stockholm through the rolling country that Linnaeus loved, the crystal summer sunshine fell on red buildings and neatly draped haystacks. Yarrow and alchemilla and yellow and white bedstraw bloomed along the roadsides, and white birches gleamed against the dark pines.

—HELEN BATCHELDER,
The Herbarist 1954

Yarrow is one of the plants whose fossil pollen has been found in burial caves of Neanderthal man. The cave findings . . . are of the period of elementary paintings dating back sixty thousand years.

—GERTRUDE B. FOSTER,
The Herb Grower

* * *

To sniff a flowering yarrow picked from the roadside on a country walk renews one's vigor for the next half mile.

—ANNIE BURNHAM CARTER

* * *

There a magic drink they gave him,
Made of Nahma-wusk, the spearmint,
And Wabeno-wusk, the yarrow,
Roots of power, and herbs of healing;
Beat their drums, and shook their rattles;
Chanted singly and in chorus. . . .

—HENRY WADSWORTH LONGFELLOW,
from "The Song of Hiawatha"

Poems of Friendship

A GARDEN BASKET

Here's garden basket, left beside your door,
With herbs to scent and flavor and to please—
That fragrant sprig, perhaps Titania wore,
While Legions and Crusaders carried these.
The leaves are messages from ancient lore,
And flowers charm a humming of the bees!

—ELISABETH W. MORSS

GIVING IS A HAPPINESS

I know someone who visits friends,
A basket at her side,
    replete with portions of her heart,
    and joy her hands provide.

She'll bring a freshly minted tea,
    perhaps a book or two,
    and jam she made one summer day,
    a daffodil she grew.
For giving is a happiness
    that spreads from just a start
    by someone with a basketful
    of treasures from the heart.

—VIRGINIA COVEY BOSWELL

BASKETS HOLD TOYS

Baskets hold toys—
   and puppies and kittens;
Baskets hold fruit—
   and sewing and mittens.
But a basket of herbs
   gathered especially for you,
Each with a message,
   some old and some new,
Is a basket of love
   from beginning to end,
A sweet-scented basket
   one gives to a friend.
      —DEBORAH WEBSTER GREELEY

MESSAGE OF THE HERBS IN A BRIDE'S BOUQUET

God's blessing is in the beauty of a flower—
And sanctifies it for a marriage dower.
The flowers in your bouquet are not by chance
But chosen for their rich significance.

The message of Chrysanthemum to youth
Is love; of white Chrysanthemum is truth;
Of Mint 'tis virtue; and of other kinds
The meaning is "the marriage of true minds."
Gray Artemisia is here to say
It hopes you may not weary on your way.
Balm brings you sympathy and Marjoram joy,

Both in full measure and without alloy;
While constancy's the soul of southernwood,
Sage is long life, and Thyme is courage good.
Sweet Woodruff augurs well for health—
A blessing richer far than wealth.
The Rose brings love in pure emotion,
While Lavender means deep devotion.
Herb of sweet omen, Rosemary conveys
Affection and remembrance all your days.

In all there's love, undying love and true,
That you've inspired in him who's guarding you
Upon the road you'll journey on together
With joyful hearts for any kind of weather.
So as you take your place, a bride,
Your chosen life-mate close beside,
May Heaven and Earth and Man combine
To keep these blessings ever thine,
And give you strength to do your part
With ready hand and loyal heart.

—RACHEL PAGE ELLIOTT

* * *

The gardener's year ends and is remembered in wreaths of fresh or dried
herbs, their fragrant beauty shared.

A FRIENDSHIP WREATH

Each herb that to this wreath its fragrance lends
Conveys its sweet significance to friends.
So, if with knowing heart you'll read it true,
You'll find a special message here for you.

Scan, then, the leafage, and remark each spray,
See where each scented thought is hid away;
And find release from trouble that disturbs
In the loved fragrance of these friendly herbs.
—HOLLIS WEBSTER
from "A Memory Wreath"

The Language of Herbs

*"Plants have a language of the Creator
intended for our translation"*—Louis Agassiz, 1807–1873

Agrimony	Thankfulness
Alder	Hope
Alkanet	Falseness, faithlessness
Aloe	Healing, protection, grief, bitterness, affection
Ambrosia	Love returned
Angelica	Inspiration, magic
Artemisia	(*See* Mugwort, Southernwood, Wormwood, Tarragon)
Balm, Lemon	Sympathy, rejuvenation
Basil	Good wishes, love
Bay, Sweet	Glory, reward
Beebalm, bergamot	Sweet virtues
Betony	Healing for your wounds; surprise
Bittersweet	Harmony
Borage	Courage
Box	Strength, constancy
Broom	Humility, neatness
Burdock	Touch-me-not, importunity
Burnet	A merry heart
Buttercup	Ingratitude, mockery, sarcasm
Butterfly-weed	Let-me-go

Cactus	Protection
Calendula	Grief, despair, contempt
Caraway	Do not steal
Carnation	Pride
	Red: alas for my poor heart
	White: sorrow
	Yellow: disdain
Celandine	Joys to come
Chamomile	Patience, long life, energy in adversity
Chervil	Sincerity, warms old hearts
Chives	Usefulness
Clary (Sage)	Clear vision
Clover	Dignity
	Red: industry
	White: promise
	Four-leaved: be mine, good luck
Columbine	Folly; I cannot give thee up
Coltsfoot	Justice shall be done
Comfrey	Comfort; healing
Coriander	Hidden worth
Costmary	Sweetness, preservation
Crocus, Saffron	Mirth, cheerfulness
Crown Imperial	Majesty, power
Cumin	Fidelity, avarice
Daisy	Hope, innocence
Dandelion	Depart, rustic oracle, coquetry
Dittany of Crete	Birth, passion
Dill	Preservation, good spirits
Dock	Patience

Elder	Compassion; bad luck, zealousness
Fennel	Strength, flattery, worthy of praise
Fern	Solitary, humility, frankness, sincerity
Forget-Me-Not	True love, forget me not
Foxglove	Adulation, insincerity, I am ambitious for you
Garlic	Healing, aphrodisiac
Geranium	Ivy: bridal favor
	Lemon: tranquillity; unexpected meeting
	Nutmeg: an expected meeting
	Oak-leaved: true friendship
	Rose: preference
	Scarlet: comforting, thou art changed
	Wild: steadfast piety
Germander	Facility, joyous
Goldenrod	Precaution, encouragement
Good King Henry	Goodness
Heliotrope	Eternal love, devotion
Holly	Good wishes, foresight, hope, divinity
Hollyhock	Ambition
Honesty	Honesty, honest wealth
Hops	Injustice
Horehound	Health
Hyssop	Penitence, humility, sacrifice, cleanliness
Iris	A message
Ivy	Immortality, fidelity, undying affection, friendship, marriage, continuity

Jasmine	Grace, elegance, amiability
Lady's Bedstraw	Restfulness
Lady's Mantle	Comfort, protection
Laurel	Triumph, eternity, victory, glory
Lavender	Devotion, luck, housewifely virtue, acknowledgment
Lily	Purity, modesty
Lily of the valley	Contentment, return of happiness, advent
Marigold, French	Uneasiness, jealousy, grief
Marjoram	Joy, happiness
Mignonette	Your qualities surpass your charms
Mints	Eternal refreshment, wisdom, virtue Peppermint: warmth of feeling Spearmint: sentiment
Mistletoe	Love, I surmount difficulties
Mullein	Good nature
Mugwort	Travel, happiness, tranquillity, "be not weary"
Myrtle	Love in absence, love, married bliss, weddings
Nasturtium	Patriotism, victory in battle
Narcissus	Selfishness, coldness, indifference
Nettle	Cruelty, slander
Olive	Peace
Orange flowers	Chastity, bridal festivity, purity, generosity
Oregano	Substance
Pansy	Thoughts Viola: remembrance, meditation Johnny-jump-up: happy thoughts

Parsley	Festivity
Partridgeberry	Cheer
Pennyroyal	Flee away
Peony	Magic, healing, ostentation
Pink	Resignation, pure love
	Clove pink: lasting beauty, affection
Plantain	Down-trodden
Poppy	Forgetfulness, sleep, oblivion, fertility, extravagance, ignorance, consolation
Primrose	Sadness, modest worth
Rose	Love, victory, pride
	Rosebud: confession of love
	Red: martyrdom, diffidence
	White: purity, too young to love
	Yellow: infidelity
	Pink: bashful love
Rosemary	Remembrance, love, loyalty
Rue	Grace, clear vision, disdain, pity
Sage	Wisdom, long life, esteem, immortality, domestic virtue
St. John's Wort	Superstition, animosity
Santolina	Wards off evil, many virtues
Savory	Interest, spiciness
Soapwort	Cleanliness
Southernwood	Constancy, jest
Speedwell (*Veronica*)	Fidelity
Spiderwort	Transient love, esteem
Strawberry	Perfect righteousness; perfection, foresight, good works

Sweet Cicely	Gladness
Sweet William	Gallantry, finesse
Sweet Woodruff	Humility
Tansy	Hostile thoughts
Tarragon	Lasting interest, appeal, seduction
Teasel	Misanthropy, importunity
Thistle	Never forget, earthly sorrow and sin, austerity
Thorn	Minor sins
Thrift	Sympathy
Thyme	Activity, bravery, courage, strength
Verbena, Lemon	Delicacy of feeling, enchantment
Violet	Humility, modesty, devotion, faithfulness
Woodbine	Fraternal love
Wormwood	Absence, displeasure, bitterness
Yarrow	Warmth, health, cure for heartache
Yew	Immortality, sorrow

Some Sources Consulted for Meanings
In The Language of Herbs

Baker, Margaret, DISCOVERING THE FOLKLORE OF PLANTS, 1969

Burke, Mrs. L., THE COLOURED LANGUAGE OF FLOWERS, George Routledge & Sons

Edgardton, Miss S. C., THE FLOWER VASE, Powers & Bagley, 1844
FABLES OF FLORA, Benjamin B. Mussey, 1844

Ferguson, George, SIGNS & SYMBOLS IN CHRISTIAN ART, Oxford University Press, 1954

Foster, Gertrude B., HERBS FOR A NOSEGAY, Privately published

Friend, Rev. Hilderic, FLOWERS AND FLOWER LORE, 1886

Greeley, Deborah Webster, THE JOY & SYMBOLISM OF HERBS AND HOLIDAY GREENS, Privately published

Greenaway, Kate, THE LANGUAGE OF FLOWERS

Grieve, Mrs. M., A MODERN HERBAL, Hafner Publishing Co., 1967

Hale, Sarah Josepha, FLORA'S INTERPRETER, Benjamin B. Mussey, 1848

Lehner, Johanna, and Ernst, FOLKLORE AND SYMBOLISM OF FLOWERS, PLANTS AND TREES, Tudor Publishing Co., 1960

Muenscher, Walter C. and Myron A. Rich, GARDEN SPICE & WILD POT-HERBS, Cornell University Press, 1955

Schafer, Violet, HERBCRAFT: A COMPENDIUM OF MYTHS, ROMANCE AND COMMON SENSE

Sigourney, Mrs. L. H. THE VOICE OF FLOWERS, H. S. Parsons Co., 1847

Waterman, Catherine H., FLORA'S LEXICON, Hooker & Agnew, 1841

Welsh, Charles, THE LANGUAGE, SENTIMENT AND POETRY OF FLOWERS, Platt & Peck, 1912

Bibliographical References

The New England Unit of The Herb Society of America, Inc., acknowledges and thanks the authors, publishers and agents whose talent, cooperation and permission to reprint have helped to make this book possible. All care has been taken to trace the origin and ownership, to obtain permission where applicable and to make appropriate acknowledgment of quotations.

Adams, Charles G.	"The Spanish Influence in California," from PIONEER AMERICAN GARDENING, edited by Elvenia Slosson, 1951, Coward, McCann & Geoghegan, Inc.
Agassiz, Louis	Quotation from notes of Helen Noyes Webster
Ammons, A. R.	DIVERSIFICATIONS, W. W. Norton, 1975
Anderson, Edgar	P. 78, PLANTS, MAN AND LIFE, Little, Brown & Co., 1952; pp. 21, 118, *The Herbarist*, 1936
Anonymous	P. 47, *Harvard Today*, Spring 1976; p. 87, Source Unknown, an often-quoted rhyme; p. 115, "E. A.," *Around the Year with Herbs*, 1942; p. 152, *The Herbarist*, 1956; p. 152, From Traveller's Notebook, *The Herbarist*, 1950
Baker, George P.	1925 newspaper clipping; source unknown
Batchelder, Helen T.	P. 13, *The Herbarist*, 1964; p. 161, *The Herbarist*, 1954
Beston, Henry	HERBS AND THE EARTH, Doubleday & Co., Inc. c. 1935 by Henry Beston

Bone, Florence — BEST LOVED POEMS FOR AMERICAN PEOPLE, Garden City Publishing Co., 1916

Boswell, Virginia Covey — *PEO Record,* June 1971

Bradstreet, Anne — "The Prologue," 1650

Breck, Joseph — BRECK'S BOOK OF FLOWERS (a catalog), Boston, 1856

Brigham, Dorcas — *The Herbarist,* 1952

Brooklyn Botanic Gardens Handbooks — "Herbs," "Herbs and Their Ornamental Uses," "Summer Flowers for Continuing Bloom," *Plants and Gardens*

Brown, Charlotte Erichsen — HERBS IN ONTARIO, Breezy Creeks Press, 1975

Brown, John Hull — EARLY AMERICAN BEVERAGES, Charles E. Tuttle Co., Tokyo, Japan, 1966 (Receipt originally published in 1866)

Brunner, Eleanor — *The Herbarist,* 1960

Bryant, William Cullen — SENTIMENT & POETRY OF FLOWERS, Platt & Peck, 1912

Bumpus, Hale — *The Herbarist,* 1975

Burroughs, John — WORKS OF JOHN BURROUGHS, Houghton Mifflin Co., Riverside Press, 1908

Campbell, Mary Mason — P. 43, Betty Crocker's KITCHEN GARDENS, Western Publishing Co., 1971; p. 159, THE NEW ENGLAND BUTT'RY SHELF ALMANAC, Harper & Row, 1970

Carter, Annie Burnham — IN AN HERB GARDEN, Rutgers University Press, 1947

Cashmore, Edna — *The Herbarist,* 1954

Child, Mrs. Lydia Maria — THE AMERICAN FRUGAL HOUSEWIFE, Samuel S. & William Wood, 1838

Claiborne, Craig — *The Boston Herald-American,* April 6, 1978

Clark, Captain William — LEWIS & CLARK JOURNALS, 1814

Clarkson, Rosetta E. — GREEN ENCHANTMENT, The Macmillan Co., Inc., 1940

Coatsworth, Elizabeth P.   P. 23, HERE I STAY, Coward, McCann, & Geoghegan, 1938; p. 159, THE WHITE ROOM, Pantheon Books, a Division of Random House, Inc., 1958

Coffin, Robert Peter Tristram   APPLES BY OCEAN, The Macmillan Co. 1950

Cook, Eliza   THE LANGUAGE, SENTIMENT & POETRY OF FLOWERS, Platt & Peck Co., 1912

Cooke, Elizabeth Throckmorton   A FEW HERBS AND APPLES, Vantage Press, 1975

Correthers, L. Young   THESE BLOOMING HERBS, privately published, 1943

Crawford, Hester Mettler   *The Potomac Herb Journal*; p. 86, *The Herbarist*, 1961

Cutler, Rev. Manasseh   AN ACCOUNT OF THE VEGETABLE PRODUCTIONS OF AMERICA, A TREATISE, American Academy, 1875

Dane, Nan   "A Christmas Tussie Mussie," gift poem sent to Helen Noyes Webster, 1931

De Sounin, Leonia   MAGIC IN HERBS, William Morrow & Co., 1941

Dickinson, Emily   P. 47, Emily Dickinson Centenary Edition, Little, Brown & Co., 1930; THE POEMS OF EMILY DICKINSON, edited by Martha Dickinson Bianchi & Alfred Leete Hampson, Little, Brown & Co., 1930

Dowden, Anne Ophelia   WILD GREEN THINGS IN THE CITY, Thomas Y. Crowell & Co., 1972

Downing, Marjorie   "Johnny Appleseed," from PIONEER AMERICAN GARDENING edited by Elvenia Slosson, Coward, McCann & Geoghegan, Inc., 1951

Duerr, Sidney   *The Herbarist*, 1965

Dunbar, Paul Lawrence   COMPLETE POEMS OF PAUL LAWRENCE DUNBAR, Dodd, Mead & Co., 1941

Earle, Alice Morse   OLD TIME GARDENS, The Macmillan Co., 1901

Edgarton, Miss S. C. THE FABLES OF FLORA, 1884
Elliott, Rachel Page Unpublished Poem
Erichsen-Brown, Charlotte See Brown, Charlotte Erichsen-
Farjeon, Eleanor POEMS FOR CHILDREN, J. B. Lippincott, 1951
Ferguson, George SIGNS & SYMBOLS IN CHRISTIAN ART, Oxford University Press, 1954

Field, Rachel COLLECTED POEMS, The Macmillan Co., 1930
Fitton, Miss "Conversations on Botany," 1817
Flagg, Wilson THE BIRDS AND SEASONS OF NEW ENGLAND, 1875
Flora's Interpreter Joseph Mussey & Co., Boston, 1848
Foley, Daniel J. THE CHRISTMAS TREE, Chilton Co., 1968; and Priscilla S. Lord: AN EASTER GARLAND, Chilton Co., 1963

Foster, Gertrude B. P. 14, 11, HERBS FOR EVERY GARDEN, E. P. Dutton & Co., 1973; pp. 32, 140, *The Herbarist*, 1968; THE HERB GROWER, 1976

Fox, Helen Morgenthau GARDENING WITH HERBS, The Macmillan Co., 1933
Fredman, Katherine I. and H. B. *The Potomac Herb Journal*, 1970

Frost, Robert THE POETRY OF ROBERT FROST, E. C. Latham, Editor; c. 1956 by Robert Frost; c. 1928, 1969 and reprinted by permission of Holt, Rinehart and Winston

Gissing, George *The Herbarist*, 1956
Gordon, Jean PAGEANT OF THE ROSE, Harper & Row, Publishers, Inc., 1952

Gray, Josephine *The Potomac Herb Journal*
Greeley, Deborah Webster Pp. 154, 164, Unpublished poems
Hale, Sarah Josepha FLORA'S INTERPRETER, Boston, 1848
Hamlin, Charles E. HAMLIN'S FORMULA, or EVERY DRUGGIST HIS OWN PERFUMER, Edward B. Read & Son, 1885

Harte, Bret "A Newport Romance," THE POETICAL WORKS OF BRET HARTE, Houghton Mifflin Co., 1870

Hawthorne, Nathaniel THE SCARLET LETTER, The Tichnor Co., 1858

Hayward, Anne G. *The Herbarist*, 1963

Hazard, Caroline SONGS IN THE SUN, Houghton Mifflin Co., 1927

Herbarist, The Published annually by The Herb Society of America Inc., 1935–1977 issues

Hickernell, Marguerite H. and Brewer, Ella W. ADAM'S HERBS, Herb-Lore, 1947

Hollingsworth, Buckner FLOWER CHRONICLES: GARDENING IN MAIN STREET, Rutgers University Press

Hopkins, Gerald Manley THE INDIGO BUNTING, by Vincent Sheean, Shocken Books, 1973

Hume, H. Harold HOLLIES, The Macmillan Co., Inc., 1953

Jefferson, Thomas THE GARDEN BOOK, annotated by Edwin Morris Betts, American Philosophical Society

Jenkins, Gladys Unpublished poems

Jewett, Sarah Orne COUNTRY OF THE POINTED FIRS, Houghton Mifflin Co., 1919

Jones, Dorothy Bovée THE HERB GARDEN, Dorrance & Co., 1972; p. 38, *The Herbarist*, 1962; p. 119, *The Herbarist*, 1958; p. 125, *The Herbarist*, 1961

Jyurovat, Genevieve G. *The Herbarist*, 1973

Langdon, Eustella PIONEER GARDENS AT BLACK CREEK PIONEER VILLAGE, Holt, Rinehart & Winston, 1972

Lawrence, Elizabeth A SOUTHERN GARDEN, University of North Carolina Press

Lee, Marion MUSIC MAKERS ANTHOLOGY, Bernard Ackerman, 1945

Leighton, Ann EARLY AMERICAN GARDENS, Houghton Mifflin Co., 1970

Lewis, Meriwether JOURNALS OF LEWIS & CLARK, 1814

Longfellow, Henry Wadsworth "Tales of a Wayside Inn," "The Goblet of Life," "Hiawatha"; THE COMPLETE POETICAL WORKS OF HENRY WADSWORTH LONGFELLOW, Houghton Mifflin Co., 1902

Lord, Priscilla Sawyer — P. 89, from an 18th-century family receipt book; p. 93, *The Potomac Herb Journal*; and Daniel J. Foley: p. 149, AN EASTER GARLAND, 1963; and Virginia Clegg Gamage, pp. 79, 123, MARBLEHEAD, THE SPIRIT OF '76 LIVES HERE, Chilton, Co., 1972; pp. 33, 65, 137, "Herbs and Their Ornamental Uses," PLANTS AND GARDENS, Brooklyn Botanic Gardens, vol. 28, No. 1, 1972; p. 86, "Summer Flowers for Continuing Bloom," PLANTS AND GARDENS, Brooklyn Botanic Gardens, vol. 24, No. 1, 1968.

Loveman, Robert — "April Rain," Harper's Monthly Magazine, 1901

Lowell, Amy — BALLADS FOR SALE, Houghton Mifflin Co., 1957

Lowell, James Russell — THE LANGUAGE OF FLOWERS, Platt & Peck, 1912

Mary Margaret, Sister O.C.D. — *The Herbarist*, 1967

McNaughton, Helen — PIONEER AMERICAN GARDENING, Elvenia Slosson, editor, Coward, McCann & Geoghegan, 1951

Mason, General John — THOMAS JEFFERSON'S GARDEN BOOK, American Philosophical Society, 1944

Mercatante, Anthony S. — THE MAGIC GARDEN, Harper & Row, Inc., 1976

Millay, Edna St. Vincent — COLLECTED POEMS, Harper & Row, Inc., (by permission of Norma Millay Ellis); p. 149, THIS SINGING WORLD, Harcourt Brace, 1947; pp. 34, 94, THE INDIGO BUNTING, by Vincent Sheean, Shocken Books, 1973

Miller, Amy Bess — SHAKER HERBS, A HISTORY AND A COMPENDIUM, Clarkson N. Potter, Inc., 1976

Miller, Mary Rogers — THE BROOK BOOK, Doubleday Page & Co., 1902

Miloradovich, Milo — THE ART OF COOKING WITH HERBS & SPICES, Doubleday & Co., Inc., 1950

Moody, William Vaughn — POEMS, Houghton Mifflin Co., 1901

Moore, Marianne — A MARIANNE MOORE READER, The Viking Press, 1954

Morss, Elisabeth W. — HERBS OF A RHYMING GARDENER, Branden Press, 1971; p. 163, Unpublished poem

Mowrer, Paul Scott   TWENTY-ONE AND SIXTY-FIVE, Wings Press, 1958

Muenscher, Walter Conrad and Myron A. Rice   GARDEN SPICE AND WILD POT-HERBS, c. 1955 by Elfriede Abbe, Cornell University Press

O'Connor, Lois   "Haiku from the Herb Garden," Unpublished

Pinney, Margaret E.   *The Herbarist*, 1974

Pond, Barbara   A SAMPLER OF WAYSIDE HERBS, The Chatham Press, Inc., 1974, illus. by E. & M. Norman; p. 52, *The Herbarist*, 1974

Potomac Herb Journal   formerly published by the Potomac Unit, The Herb Society of America, Inc.

Randolph, John   TREATISE ON GARDENING, 1765–1770, Williamsburg, Virginia

Randolph, Mrs. Mary   THE VIRGINIA HOUSEWIFE OR METHODICAL COOK, Hurst & Co., Publishers, 1813

Rawson, Marion Nicholl   FROM HERE TO YENDER, E. P. Dutton & Co., 1932

Reese, Lizette Woodworth   SELECTED POEMS, George H. Doran Co., 1926

Richardson, Mayre B.   *The Herbarist*, 1957

Romig, Edna Davis   FLASH OF WINGS, Johnson Publishing Co., 1967

Saunders, Mira Cullin   *The Herbarist*, 1967

Simmons, Adelma G.   HERB GARDENING IN FIVE SEASONS, D. Van Nostrand Co., 1964; p. 100, *The Herbarist*, 1968

Simmons, Amelia   AMERICAN COOKERY, Hartford, 1796, the first American cookbook

Sheean, Vincent   THE INDIGO BUNTING, Schocken Books, 1973, permission of Norma Millay Ellis

Shepard, Odell   HOME THOUGHTS, Houghton Mifflin Co., 1923

Slosson, Elvenia   Editor, PIONEER AMERICAN GARDENING, Coward, McCann & Geoghegan, Inc., 1951

Smith, Georgiana Reynolds   TABLE DECORATION YESTERDAY, TODAY, & TOMORROW, Charles E. Tuttle Co., Tokyo, 1968

Smith, Mrs. Samuel Harrison   THOMAS JEFFERSON'S GARDEN BOOK, American Philosophical Society, 1944

Stephens, Helen S.   *The Herbarist*, 1966

Strayer, Nanette M.   *The Herbarist*, 1964

Acknowledgments

"Insouciance" by A. R. Ammons, from DIVERSIFICATIONS, copyright A. R. Ammons 1975, by permission of W. W. Norton & Co., Inc., publisher.

Excerpts from *Herbs and the Earth*, by Henry Beston, copyright 1935 by Henry Beston, by permission of Doubleday & Co., Inc.

From *Betty Crocker's Kitchen Gardens*, by Mary Mason Campbell, copyright 1971 by Western Publishing Co., Inc., used by permission of the publisher.

Pantheon Books, a Division of Random House, Inc., permission to quote from *The White Room* by Elizabeth Coatsworth, copyright Pantheon Books.

Elizabeth T. Cooke, for permission to quote from her *A Few Herbs and Apples*, her material on Bouncing Bet.

Oxford University Press, New York, N.Y., publishers, for permission to quote from *Signs and Symbols in Christian Art*, by George Ferguson.

Mortimer J. Fox, for permission to quote from the book by Helen Morgenthaux Fox, *Gardening With Herbs*.

"The Rose Family," from *The Poetry of Robert Frost*, edited by Edward Connery Lathem, copyright 1928, 1969 by Holt, Rinehart and Winston, copyright 1956 by Robert Frost; reprinted by permission of Holt, Rinehart and Winston, publishers.

Macmillan Publishing Co., Inc., for permission to quote from *Hollies*, by H. Harold Hume, copyright 1953 by Macmillan Publishing Co., Inc.

University of North Carolina Press, Chapel Hill, for permission to quote from *A Southern Garden* by Elizabeth Lawrence.

Chilton Book Company, for permission to quote from *Marblehead: The Spirit of '76 Lives Here,* by Priscilla S. Lord and Virginia Clegg Gamage; and from *An Easter Garland,* by Priscilla S. Lord and Daniel J. Foley.

Harper & Row, Publishers, Inc., for permission to quote from The Magic Garden: *The Myth and Folklore of Flowers, Plants, Trees and Herbs,* by Anthony S. Mercatante, published and copyrighted in 1976 by Harper & Row, Publishers, Inc.

Norma Millay Ellis, for permission to quote as follows from the work of Edna St. Vincent Millay: The material on p. 157 from *Collected Poems,* Harper & Row, copyright 1921, 1923, 1948, 1951, and 1954, by Edna St. Vincent Millay and Norma Millay Ellis; the material on pp. 34 and 94 from *Indigo Bunting* by Vincent Sheean, published by Shocken Books, 1973; p. 149 from *This Singing World*, Harcourt, Brace Co., 1947.

Excerpt from *The Art of Cooking with Herbs and Spices,* by Milo Miloradovich, copyright 1950 by Milo Miloradovich, reprinted by permission of Doubleday & Co., Inc.

Verses by Elisabeth W. Morss from her book *Herbs of a Rhyming Gardener,* copyright 1971 by Branden Press, Inc., for permission to quote, from Branden Press, Inc.

Viking Penguin Inc., for permission to quote "Rosemary," from *The Complete Poems of Marianne Moore,* copyright 1954 by Marianne Moore.

Cornell University Press, for permission to quote from *Garden Spice and Wild Pot-Herbs*, by Walter C. Muenscher and Myron A. Rice, copyright 1955 by Elfriede Abbe.

Coward, McCann & Geoghegan, Inc., permission to quote from *Pioneer American Gardening*, edited by Elvenia Slosson, copyright 1951 by Elvenia Slosson.

Charles E. Tuttle Co., Inc., Tokyo, as publishers, permission to quote from *Table Decoration Yesterday, Today & Tomorrow*, by Georgiana Reynolds Smith.

E. B. White, permission to quote the material on goldenrod from the book of his wife, Katharine S. White, *Onward and Upward in the Garden*.